KING OF RUIN

LORDS OF LAS VEGAS

TAMMY ANDRESEN

❀ Created with Vellum

STALK ME LIKE AN ALPHA!

Join my newsletter to get all the latest updates!

Tammy's Newsletter

And follow me everywhere else for teasers, giveaway, book news and fun!

www.authortammyandresen.com
www.facebook.com/authortammyandresen
www.instagram.com/tammyandresen
https://www.tiktok.com/@lordsoflasvegas
www://amazon.com/authortammyandresen

KING OF RUIN

A scheming billionaire perched on the brink of dominance.

A vulnerable visually impaired woman caught in a war…

Cold

Calculating

Ruthless

A king

Roman Kincaid is everything I'm not… He's a king. A god among men.

I'm just the blind girl who hides from the world.

But despite being visually impaired, and the caretaker of every wounded animal that comes my way, it does not exempt me from catching his notice.

I can't make out the color of his eyes, but I can still feel their heat.

Because I've got something he wants. A postage stamp lot in the heart of Las Vegas.

But the one thing that's mine, is the very thing he needs.

And there isn't anything he won't do to get it.

He's not the only one.

His enemies want it too. Which means I'm caught in their war.

I've no choice but to ask the man who frightens me more than any other to keep me safe.

And just because there is an attraction that simmers between us, that doesn't make Roman my protector. Or a good guy.

He is NOT a hero.

He is a predator.

And I am his…

Prey.

CHAPTER ONE

Roman

The blades of the helicopter are still whirring over my head as I exit the chopper at the top of Kincaid Tower. My cousin Luke is just behind me.

What a fucking day.

From our vantage point, I can see all the lights of Vegas spread out before us. The city glitzes and shimmers like the grand illusion that it is. Meant to be an oasis, it's just as lethal as the desert beyond.

I'd hoped to get back sooner.

But we'd had Nia and Jake to see off on their trip to the Keys, and then there had been the car to deal with….

It takes a bit of time to dispose of a burnt-out wreck with bullet holes.

And of course, there was the body…

I scrub a hand through my hair as Luke pushes a button on his phone, unlocking the rooftop door to the private elevator.

"I got seven calls while we were in flight," he growls out as the door opens and we step into the elevator.

"Any of them the police?" I ask, my eyes closing as I lean against the wall, exhaustion pulling at my limbs.

"No. Just the fucking building inspector, the lead architect, and the foreman of the construction crew. Fuck me. Somethings royally fucked up, I'm sure."

The moment the doors slide open to the conference room, he's got his phone to his ear, snarling words I only half listen to as I pour myself a glass of scotch from the bar at the far end of the room.

In theory, my brothers, my cousin Luke, my uncle Jake, and I are the five owners of a successful real estate enterprise.

But we are also the five fingers of a fist, punching at anyone who gets in our way.

And no one gets to where we are without getting his hands dirty.

I take a large swallow of the drink and then another, I don't love these days. The days where I'm not in the boardroom but fighting off the Italian Mafia as they try to take what is ours with guns instead of corporate mergers.

But either way, we do what we have to do to stay on top.

My phone rings, my brother Mason's name popping up on the screen. I take another swallow and pick up. "Mason."

"What the fuck happened today?"

"Toni's dead, Jake is wounded, and Nia is on the war path." And then I finish the glass and pour another.

"Toni's dead?"

"Yeah. Tweedledee and Tweedledum Vendetti were with him, though, and they both got away."

"Vigo and Vincent are problems we're going to need to solve soon. Tell me about Nia."

"I think the Vendetti twins are going to be the much easier discussion."

Mason sighs. "Tell me about Nia anyway."

"Our new aunt," I say with a snort because, while Jake is pushing forty, Nia is younger than all of us. Why he'd want a woman like that, a woman who actually calls him Daddy, is beyond me. "Would like some recompense from Gris Smith. In her words, she's paid a hefty price to become part of this family. And Jake just had to kill her father to keep her, and us, safe. But she feels that Gris has been all gain and no pain after the way he set her up and it's time he put his skin on the line too. She's not wrong."

Mason grunts. "Should have seen that one coming."

And that's why Mason is our fearless leader. He rarely misses a move and blames himself when he does. "Her exact words to Gris's brother, Tris, were, and I'm quoting, 'I'm a Mafia princess who is now a queen of Vegas. You didn't think what your brother did was going to go unpunished?'"

"What did Jake say?" Mason asks, not commenting on Nia at all. He's calculating the damage and how to spin this to our advantage, I know it.

"He said, 'Give him hell, baby girl.'" I repeat. Jake was completely behind his woman. Then again, Jake has been hooked about as deeply as a man can be.

She's not so vulnerable anymore. Jake has gone about eliminating her problems one body at a time.

Hence why I was on clean-up duty today.

"And Triston Smith? What was his response?"

"It seems like he's going to make his brother pay whatever price Nia demands."

"She's a businesswoman underneath the bombshell exterior," Mason murmurs. "She negotiated with me like a pro. And I am a man with a lot of experience when it comes to creating deals."

"That is true." I take another swallow, as I consider. Mason sounds like he's going to support Nia too. Was he looking for an excuse to back out of his deal with the Brits? Gris and Tris are new players in Vegas, having come from London to own a piece of the American dream.

"But honestly, Gris is the steel in the group. Not Triston. This could mean war." I hear Mason scratch his chin. "Gris is a threat to us, I've always known it. We just can't afford another enemy right now."

The idea of another party to fight makes me tired.

"Shit. I'm getting a text from Jake now." He pauses, likely reading the message.

"He says that Nia's decided on her demand of the Smiths.... She wants to put our casino security man in charge of his casinos too. Eyes and ears right on every one of their floors."

I pull the phone away from my ear and stare at it. Christ. It's a brilliant plan. "Wow," I mutter.

"I know. Turns out, our young little princess is making us stronger."

"Remind me not to piss her off," I respond, though I know I pissed her off already. She was our enemy's daughter and I don't do well with women who have a lot of baggage.

In my defense, my mother died when I was young. Just eleven. Car accident. If you can call being fall-down drunk and then driving an accident. My hand clenches around my phone as I bring my glass back to my lips.

I take another swallow of my second drink, knowing I ought to slow down. But the past few days have unsettled some careful balance I usually keep.

"Fuck," Luke yells from the next room, loud enough that Mason hears him too.

"What's happening?" Mason asks.

Instead of answering, I switch the phone to speaker and cross the conference room to the adjoining meeting room.

Luke is standing by the windows, his back stiff and straight, his jaw clenched in hard lines. "How much did you offer her?" he asks in clipped tones as he speaks into his phone.

My brow furrows as I cock my head and listen.

"And she didn't take it?"

Mason is silent, surely listening too.

"Make her another offer, double it." Luke's hand slices through the air like he'd like to cut all this bullshit.

"Why wouldn't she want that kind of money?" He looks back at me, his brow furrowed in an angry line as he listens to the speaker on the other end of the phone. "Are you fucking kidding me?" He spits.

"What's wrong?" I finally ask, not that he answers.

"Tell me you're researching her. Find a weakness, find a way to make sure she sells." And then he hangs up.

I wait, not one to repeat myself as he drops his phone in his pocket and scrubs his face.

Letting out a long breath of air, he finally grunts. "Problem with the tunnel."

"What problem?" Mason asks.

Luke eyes my phone like I've betrayed him. Did he not want Mason to hear this? That's too bad. We don't keep secrets from each other.

"The problem is that there aren't enough ventilation vents in the tunnel and the place they've requested we add one, is underneath the land of a small nonprofit animal sanctuary."

Small animal sanctuary? In the city?

"Judging by what I heard," Mason clears his throat. "Offers have been made, but she's refusing to part with the land?"

"That's right," Luke nods, looking at me with a pained expression that tells me there is more that Luke isn't sharing.

I set down my glass and scrub a hand across my jaw. "We'll take a look at the property. See what size it is, what facilities she's got. My guess is if we offered a larger parcel with more amenities somewhere else, she'd take that deal."

Luke's eyes light up.

"I agree," Mason rumbles. "The sooner the better. We could do with a few less problems."

We certainly could.

I hang up with Mason and pick up my glass, draining the drink. "First thing tomorrow?" I ask, wishing for nothing more than the bliss of my quiet apartment and the comfort of my bed.

Luke shakes his head. "I'm not sleeping tonight. I think I'll go now."

"You can't show up at a woman's place at one in the morning without ending up in a jail cell."

"I just want to do a drive by and it's a business, not a home."

I scowl. "I'm going to bed, and I'm not picking up my phone, so if you end up in jail, I'm not bailing you out tonight. You're sleeping with the drunks."

"You're not coming with me?" Luke asks with a frown. "I could use your eyes on this one. Without the vent, the project will be stalled for months. Our first permits are running out the end of this week."

That was what he didn't tell Mason. The two of them have a weird dynamic. Mason is my actual brother. Luke is the cousin that is like a brother. But the two of them…it's different. Mason was long gone by the time I moved in with Luke. Off at school.

I mutter several curses because that's Luke. Leaving out important information and running things down to the wire. "I hate you right now."

"But you'll come?"

I let out a long breath of air as I look down at the second glass of scotch I just finished.

Maybe it's the drinks, or the hellish day, but a sense of dread fills me. "Fine. Asshole."

"Thanks, dickhead."

He strides toward the elevator. "I'll drive."

I set down the glass and follow behind him. "What do we know about this woman?"

"She's some hippie, I think. She takes the birds that get wounded running into the skyscrapers and doctors them or some shit. There can't be any money in it."

This is decent information. She's probably not motivated by our offer and she'll want to be close to the city. "She probably doesn't care about money, Luke. People who start non-profits sometimes don't." Unless they use them to launder. Which is an interesting possibility. "This hippie have a name?"

"Maddie Reid." Luke presses the button at least a dozen times as we wait for the doors to open. "It's a tiny tenth of an acre parcel but she's refusing to sell, despite the offer being four times the value of the property."

I frown as I take in that particular piece of information. "Either she's crazy or she's got some ulterior motive." I'll keep my theories to myself until I know more.

Luke shakes his head. "I agree. Which is why I want to gather a bit of information where I can assess the property without being observed."

The elevator opens and I give him a long glare as we step in. "I've had enough shady dealings for today."

"I'm not going to be shady." He doesn't meet my eye as he leans casually against the wall.

"Bullshit." Luke is the king of looking carefree and charming. It's an act.

"Ok, I'm not going to get caught. Besides, we both know a woman like that does not have an alarm or cameras."

I shake my head, knowing I'm going to regret this as the elevator stops at the garage and we walk toward Luke's Ferrari.

The drive is short, her small parcel right in the heart of the city. How she's kept it for this long without selling is rather impressive. She must have had lots of offers as new Vegas has built up around her. Why not cash out?

We get out of the car, the flickering streetlights only making me more certain I've made a mistake. The alcohol is taking effect, and my senses are dulled as I survey the street. We're on the back side of several casinos where traffic is lighter.

But it's late and it's a good spot for trouble.

I turn back to look at the lot. The property is protected by six-foot-high brick walls, not that Luke cares.

Before I've said a word, he takes a three-step running leap and vaults over the top. "You're a billionaire who wears a suit most days. What the fuck are you doing?"

"I'm a man who gets the job done," he calls from the other side of the wall. "And we both know I like wearing jeans way more than I like suits."

Several birds squawk in response and I roll my eyes. "What you're doing is your best to get arrested."

But I stop talking, letting him do his thing as I watch the street.

I do manage to note that the walled yard is attached to a stucco building that looks like it might be a two-family residence. Another Vegas oddity.

No lights are on inside, but I have this moment of unease. Does Madison live there? Is that why she won't sell?

I cock my head to the side. "Luke," I rumble out in a rough whisper. I'm liking this less and less.

He hops back over the wall. "She's got about thirty birds and a few squirrels. That's what's holding up our billion-dollar project. A few parakeets."

"Parakeets don't fly into buildings, they live inside them around here," I answer automatically, not even looking at him. Something isn't right. I can feel it.

"Seriously, though. Why won't she sell?"

That's when I see the headlights coming around the corner. I step back into the shadow of the wall, my arm flinging out, to push Luke back too.

"Fuck," he mutters as the car not only comes toward us but stops right in front of the house.

"You packing?" I ask, realizing that I'm not.

"No," he spits. "Shit. I ditched my gun at the office."

We're hidden but his car is in plain view, parked just in front of the Maserati that just pulled up.

The driver, a large muscular man, gets out of the car and opens the rear door behind him, helping another person from the car.

There is something familiar about the guy, and I lean closer. If I'd skipped the scotch, I'm sure I'd already know what's making the hair on the back of my neck stand up.

I eye the second, smaller person. Even in this light, I catch the flash of long blonde hair as the man slips a hand around her waist, walking her toward the door.

"Fuck me, that's Vigo Vendetti," Luke mutters.

The passenger door opens, and when the streetlight catches the second man, I know that Luke is correct. It's Vigo's brother, Vincent

Vendetti, who steps out onto the sidewalk. He takes a long look at Luke's car, before he starts walking straight toward us.

This is bad.

The Vendettis are the unhinged nephews of the man we killed today. And if they realize that the Ferrari is Luke's, they've got us right where they want us...

I lean closer to the wall, my jaw hard as granite. "What do you want to do?"

I hear Luke growl. "We can make a break for the car, or we can..."

But Vincent's scanning the area and I swear he sees me, our eyes locking.

My hand comes to my chest, feeling the bullet proof layer of protection I've been wearing since this morning.

It only takes a second for Vincent to reach behind him and pull out a pistol.

I barely hear the two pops before I feel the bullet strike my upper chest. I look over just in time to see Luke go down...

CHAPTER TWO

MADDIE

FOUR HOURS EARLIER...

"I DON'T DATE," I mutter to my best friend, Lucia, as she applies a brush of mascara to my lashes.

I can do the task myself. A person can feel the bend of their lashes on the lid. And with good light, I can see enough to not completely hack the job if I lean really close to the mirror.

My vision is just poor enough to make me legally blind, but I'm not sightless.

"I'm well aware of your dating preferences," Lucia says as she dips the brush into the bottle, completing my makeup. "But you can't stay here all day, every day, with no company other than birds and a few squirrels."

"Why not?" I grump, even though I know she's probably right. Granted, I have her, and the Amazon delivery guy and I are pretty tight. And by that, I mean we talk occasionally when he delivers a package.

Though, technically, he has asked me out twice. And for someone like me, dating a delivery guy would have real advantages…

But since my grandmother's death, I've really withdrawn, and Lucia has taken it upon herself to push me out of my funk.

Which is why she dragged me to some swanky bar last week because I needed to "get out" and see the world beyond my little walled garden. I'd reluctantly agreed and somehow managed to acquire a date with Vigo Vendetti.

He talks like a gangster. His tone is all male bravado, which I don't like at all, but his touch on my elbow was gentle enough.

And when he'd asked, I'd been about to say no when Lucia had hissed in my ear. "He's hot. Like hot, hot."

I didn't need her to tell me. I could see the outline of his muscular frame, smell his expensive cologne.

Even I'd seen the rough, masculine cut of his jaw, and so, with a sigh, knowing Lucia wouldn't leave me alone if I said no, I'd accepted his invitation.

Now, here I was, in a dress, with mascara on, seriously regretting allowing Lucia to bully me into this.

"Maybe I should put a few more curls in your hair. It's getting a little flat." She's close enough, I see her frown as she inspects my blonde coif.

I shake my head. My hair is thick enough but it's always been really soft and silky so it's never held a curl. A fact I tried to tell her before she broke out the curling iron. "Leave it," I say. "I already told you, it's not going to stay."

She makes that dissatisfied sound she usually reserves for surgery, but the curling iron clinks back down on the bathroom countertop.

"I just want you to look…"

I reach for her hand, holding her fingertips in my palm. Lucia is a veterinarian, her husband is her assistant. I know in her heart she thinks I'd be better off if I were married too. Which I appreciate.

Honestly though, I'd be a lot for any guy to take on. And I'm not even talking about my sight. Well, I am pretty much talking about my lack of sight.

But I've also got a menagerie of pets that I love but would drive any other person to distraction. "Lucia. These things can't be forced."

"I know. I know you're right," she sighs, her fingers flexing against my palm. "But some effort might help."

I let go of her hand and then reach up to fluff my strands of hair. The clock in the hall chimes out nine, which means Vigo will be here any minute.

It's the first date I've ever had that started after seven. Granted, I think the last time I went out with a guy was sophomore year of college. Was that really two years ago? Lucia might be right. I do need to get out.

But it's so tough when you're different. Not a lot of guys even want to date someone like me. And once I get past that hurdle…my other sinking point surfaces. The guy from sophomore year and I had gone out a few times, had a nice time in the back of his car until I'd confessed that I was a virgin. The night had ended early and he didn't ask me out again.

I get it.

Honestly, I'm kind of hoping for different results from Vigo. I'm almost twenty-two and haven't even managed to go all the way. I don't really see Vigo as boyfriend material, but I bet he'd be all right for getting rid of my virginity.

After that…

I'm not even sure I want the pressure of dating. It has always been much safer to keep my little animals as company.

People are usually so disappointing. Or maybe I just disappoint them.

Not Lucia, of course. Despite my grumpiness at being forced into this date, she is one of the rare people I can count on to be a standout person and friend.

Which is why I just allowed her to doll me up like a harlot.

And not her husband, Josh. He's a really good guy who is crazy supportive of his wife. He's sitting out on my couch now, watching a baseball game, while he waits for Lucia to be done with my transformation.

I wish I was with him. I love baseball. Maybe because it's a slow enough game that the auditory alone makes me feel like I can see it.

Lucia reaches for something on the counter, the click of the blush case alerting me that she's about to apply even more makeup when my doorbell rings.

"Thank goodness," I sigh as I push up from the chair she's placed in my tiny bathroom.

I inherited my house from my maternal grandmother. It's a little two-story two-family, left over from a long-forgotten time in Las Vegas before the strip was built. It's my oasis in this city and my connection with one of the few other people who loved me in this world.

I hear Josh answer the door, his friendly call of hello, met with silence.

I push out of the bathroom and down the hall, tension thick in my small living room. I can get around my house no matter the light, having lived here all my life.

"Hi," I call, my voice high pitched and breathy with my own nervousness, coming to stand next to Josh and in front of Vigo.

"Who's this guy?" Vigo grunts instead of answering me. My smile dies. I like strong men. The few guys I've dated have had serious alpha vibes.

But Vigo isn't coming across alpha, he just sounds like a jerk.

"Josh, Vigo. Vigo, Josh."

"Hey, Vigo," Lucia says from behind me. "Nice to see you again." She lightly pushes me to the side, standing between me and Josh. "We should let these two crazy kids go off on their date. It's baseball night for us."

Vigo grunts but doesn't apologize to Josh or say hello to me as he turns and starts walking down the front steps...without me.

Am I supposed to follow? I sigh as I take a few steps. This isn't the most auspicious start, and I already know this isn't ending with a night in bed. Vigo is just too rough...

Too bad.

I know my own steps and I make it down them easily enough, but I can't see the car in the darkness and I've no idea which way I'm going. "Vigo?"

Maybe he won't answer. Maybe he'll just drive off. Granted, it would mean I wasted the last hour primping, but then again, I could listen to the game and eat popcorn with Josh and Lucia, which sounds way more fun than pretending my date isn't a jerk.

"Here," he says, and then his hand comes to my elbow.

Both his voice and his touch are gentle this time and I breathe out a sigh of relief as he walks me to the car and then opens the door.

I touch his hand on my arm to stop him from helping me in. "Hey, Vigo?"

"Yeah?" He asks in a half grunt as his fingers clench and unclench on my arm, his impatience clear.

Another sign he's not enjoying my company.

"We don't have to do this if you don't want."

"Do what?" he asks, and he sounds irritated again. I grimace.

"Go out." I draw in a quick breath. "I get it...dating someone like me might not be that fun. It's my fault."

He gives my arm a small squeeze, all his hectic energy gone. "I think dating a girl like you is going to be lots and lots of fun."

"How's that?" I ask, the tiniest tremor of fear moving through me. It's the word choice and the tone that make his words sound like a threat.

He pauses and I can actually feel his gaze sliding down me, his body hardening. Does he like that I'm extra vulnerable? Again, I'm all for alphas but I feel almost...unsafe. And not in the he's dangerously hot kind of way.

I hear him suck at his lip. "You're hot, Maddie."

"Oh." Heat rises in my cheeks as he opens the door and hands me in. It only takes a second for me to realize he's putting me in the backseat on the passenger's side. What the...

"Hi," a woman's voice chirps from my left. "I'm Kate."

"Hi," I answer back. There's another woman on our date?

"Hey gorgeous," another male voice says from the front. "Remember me?"

I know the voice. It's Vigo's brother, Vincent. They were together when Vigo and I met. "Is this a double date?"

A door in the front of the car closes. "Did I not mention that?" Vigo asks, sounding unconcerned.

"Nope. You didn't." But I really don't mind. In fact, it's a relief. Not being alone with Vigo will make this night so much easier.

The car speeds off and Kate asks me several questions about myself, which I mostly deflect back to her.

She's in medical school, and only visiting Vegas for the summer for an internship. She met Vincent two nights ago when she was at a restaurant alone having dinner. "I haven't made any friends here yet," she whispers with a small laugh. "It's nice to talk with another woman."

"It's so wonderful to chat with you too," I answer back, meaning it. She's been really nice.

Which makes me wonder what she's doing out with Vincent.

If Vigo goes from nice to jerk and back again, Vincent consistently reeks of giant a-hole. Like class bully vibes.

We pull up to some place with a large crowd and get out as the valet takes the keys. "Not a scratch," Vincent rumbles before he hands them over. "I fucking mean it. I will end you if anything happens to my car."

I cringe at his words and his tone.

Vigo's hand is at my elbow again and I'm whisked inside and straight to a private room, the sound of the crowd dying away as our chairs are quietly pulled out.

"Wow," Kate says in a whisper as she looks around. "I knew this would be a good dinner if I said yes. I can't even afford a spot in the dining room at this place, let alone a private room."

"Stick with me, baby," Vincent replies with enough obvious smarm to make me actually wince.

"Your friend Lucia. Where is she from?" Vigo asks from my other side.

"Boston."

"I mean, where in Italy," Vigo snorts. "She's got an Italian name."

My mouth opens and closes as I try to formulate a proper response. How was I supposed to know that's what he meant? "Umm, east coast, I think. Near San Marino."

"We're from Rome," Vigo says with pride. "Still keep in touch with family there. In fact, one of our cousins is visiting."

It's on the tip of my tongue to ask if their Italian relatives are gangsters too. I get sassy when I'm irritated, and this date is on the way to pissing me off.

But Vincent speaks first. "You should go there sometime. Sights are amazing."

Kate delicately clears her throat, as I try to hide a smile. His words don't bother me, it's difficult to consider things from other people's perspectives, but the idea of me sightseeing is amusing. "I'll keep that in mind."

The waiter arrives and Vigo and Vincent begin ordering for the table.

Kate leans closer. "What is the extent of your impairment?"

"Legally blind but only just," I reply, also used to this question.

"If you need any help tonight, just ask," she offers with a light touch to my arm.

"Thank you, Kate. I really appreciate that."

"I don't know about you," she leans closer. "But I only said yes to get a really nice dinner. They've been hard to come by lately and I could tell Vincent would spring for a quality restaurant."

I let out a very soft laugh. "I was hoping for a really good dessert," I reply with a wink.

She lets out a small gasp before she laughs too. "Oh, you're fun."

I hope I can get her number before the night is out. I don't think I'm getting another date or dessert out of my night with Vigo, but a new friend would be amazing.

I let most of my college friends go when I dropped out. Lucia is right about one thing. I've let my world get very small. But caring for my gran at the end was tough and then I was grieving. But it's time to step out into the world again.

The rest of the evening passes in much the same fashion, and I'm relieved when we load in the car to go home.

I'm certain that Vigo won't ask for an invitation in since we're with other people. If he does ask me out again, I can just say no.

I do lean over to Kate on the drive home. "Any chance you'd be interested in coffee sometime?"

"I'd love that," she whispers back as I hand her my phone and she plugs in her number.

I take the phone back, just as we pull up to the curb. I expect Vigo to open the door right away but the energy in the car shifts again. A tension fills the car as Vigo spits something in Italian to his brother and Vincent curses in return.

I barely notice when the phone slips from my fingers.

"Whose car is that?" Vincent rumbles. "Who do you know that's got a Ferrari?"

"Me?" I ask, shaking my head. "No one." People in my world don't drive sports cars. Lucia has a beat up, very old Honda Civic.

"I'll get her inside," Vigo mutters. "Don't do anything until her door is closed." And then I'm being whisked out of the car, Vigo tugging me from the seat.

"What does that mean?" Kate asks just as the door slams shut. I turn toward her, squeezing Vigo's arm.

"Kate should come in too—"

"Don't fucking move," Vincent says. I have no idea who he's talking to. Me? But I freeze at his harsh tone.

Vigo, however, tugs me forward, pulling me toward the house. I nearly trip on the sidewalk but he doesn't stop. "Key," he barks.

I pull the metal from my pocket, as I lift it up with a trembling hand. "Please." I try again. "You can leave Kate here. But she should come in with us."

"Shut up." He inserts the key in the lock and swings open the door just as two pops fill the night.

"What was..." I start to ask but his hand comes to my face.

"You see that?"

"No." I shake my head. "Just heard it. It sounded like…"

"Fireworks," he answers, before he pushes me inside the door. "I'll call you tomorrow."

And then he shuts it again.

I stand in my dark living room and listen to the sound of Vigo half yelling at Vincent as the trunk of the car opens and closes, before the car speeds away.

What the hell just happened?

The house is dark and quiet. I don't move, listening to the night. And that's when I hear it.

A low groan.

And then another.

It sounds like a wounded animal or a… man.

Reaching for the knob I slowly open the door and step outside…

CHAPTER THREE

Maddie

The groaning only grows louder.

I know the sound of a wounded soul and this one has all the markers. "Hello?" I softly whisper.

The night is so dark, I have no idea what or who I'm going to find. I can't even see the outlines of large shapes.

"Shit," I hear a deep male voice grind out. "That fucking hurt."

"What hurts?" I ask, inching closer. I reach out a hand, the feel of light wool sliding under my fingers.

Suit? If it is, it's expensive.

"Chest." he reaches for my hand, strong fingers grabbing mine as pulls my hand toward his body and places it on his torso.

I don't feel any blood and his body feels padded under my hand. Spreading my fingers out, I search for a wound and only manage to find a hole in his shirt. Definitely a dress shirt. What's a man in a suit doing outside my house on the ground?

Placing my finger lightly over the hole in his clothing, I press down. Cool metal touches my skin. "What's this?"

His fingers replace mine and the air rushes out of his lungs. "Bulletproof vest."

I draw in a quick breath because the details are stitching together. This man was shot while wearing a bulletproof vest, and Vigo and Vincent… "Who shot you?"

He groans. "Can we check my head first? It hurts like hell."

I run my hand up his chest, over the strong cords of his neck and into his hair. He's half sitting, propped against the brick wall that fences in my yard and I only need to search the softly curled strands of hair for a moment to find a giant lump forming on the back of his head. I gasp even as he winces away, in obvious pain.

"My friend could look at you," I say as I slowly reach back into his hair to explore further. "Lucia has medical training."

"Lucia?" he asks, a bitter note of cold lacing his voice. "I don't think so."

I nip at my lip, not sure what to do. "Should I call an ambulance?"

"No."

"The police?" But I already know the answer and it was a potentially dangerous question to ask. He's wearing a bulletproof vest. He was prepared to be shot, which means he…

"No police."

I sit down on the pavement, my hand still threaded in his hair. I thought Vigo seemed *like* a gangster but now I'm pretty sure that he *actually* is one. What does that make this man? "You want me to just leave you here?"

"No," he shakes his head. "For all I know, the Vendettis are coming back."

The proof that it was my date and his brother who did the shooting sits like a dead weight in my stomach. "What then?"

"We need to go inside."

My brows lift at the absurdity. "You want me to bring you into my house?"

He lets out a long breath of air. "Did you see what happened?"

"No," which is the truth, but I'm beginning to understand his line of questioning.

"Hear it?"

"I…"

He reaches for my hand. "What's your name?"

"Maddie," I whisper, not sure I should give more detail than that.

"You live here?" he asks.

"I do."

He lets out a long sigh. "Did I hear birds in your yard?"

My lips part as I try to marry that question with all events of the evening. My birds seem of no consequence… "I run a sanctuary." A topic that has been increasingly notable of late.

I've recently had several offers on the property. Kincaid Enterprises alone has made me three offers in the last three weeks. Not that I'd ever sell.

"Maddie, can we please go inside? I can assure you, that I am no danger to you, but I may be a great help. Vigo and Vincent are not men to trifle with."

He's not wrong.

I nip at my lip for another second, though. I've already figured out that I never want to see Vigo again. The question now is… is the man in front of me more or less dangerous than the one I was just with?

Why did I come out here? I shake my head, listening to him moan, how could I not?

Then again, some people would have just called 911.

But… I hear him try to push up and then slump back down, I sigh, reaching for his hand again. "Let me help you."

His arm slides around my shoulders as I bend down, and using every ounce of my strength, I get him up on his feet.

Slowly, we shuffle toward my door.

I see the vague outline of a car parked in front of my house. "Whose car is that?"

"My cousin's," he grits out.

"Where is he?"

"I don't know," he answers, glancing back. "He's gone. I blacked out for a second and when I came to…"

My heart stops in my chest because…there were two pops and two people. I remember the sound of the trunk and that Kate was in the back of the car still.

Gasping, my arm around his middle tightens.

"What's wrong?"

"Vincent's date was in the car," I whisper.

"Girlfriend?"

"No. Just a date like me. She said she went for the dinner. She—"

"Maddie."

This time, my name in his deep baritone sends a skitter of nerves shivering through me. It's a little fear but it's the good kind of fear. Like the delicious and a little dark thrill of excitement. "Yes?"

"We really should get inside."

"Right," I start toward the door again, feeling for the railing to my front steps. If only there was some moonlight.

The hard length of him is leaning heavily into me as I inch forward, reaching out my hand.

"What's wrong?" he asks.

"My eyes aren't so good," I answer, hating to admit the truth. Which is weird. I stopped being so insecure about my impairment a long time ago. "And it's really dark."

There is a pause, it's one I'm used to, one I've heard many times before, when a person recalibrates what they think about you. Feel.

My heart stutters in my chest.

What happens next is as varied as people. Some talk excessively, some misinform me of everything they know about my condition. Some retreat quickly, and others make excuses.

I hold my breath as I wait to learn how he'll treat me. For some reason, his reaction matters more than usual. "I've got the rail," he answers as he swings us around. "Step is right in front of you."

"Thank you," I answer, my voice a bit breathless as I nearly stumble up the first step. But after that one, I'm good. The familiar pattern of the stairs helps me help him, and we're inside in the next minute, the door closing behind me.

I hold his hand to lower him to the couch, then spin back, quickly locking the door.

Did I just lock the bad guy out or in?

I turn back to my...erm...guest. I flick on the lights to at least see the broad outline of him. He's spread out on the couch, long legs before him, broad shoulders taking up one whole end of the sofa.

His hair is dark, I don't know the shade, but the cut of his jaw is ridiculously perfect. Like model perfect.

I wet my lips, suddenly nervous. Looking at him now, I've got no idea what happens next. I twist my hands together, wondering if I've made a giant mistake.

I can hear my grandmother's voice. *"Always rushing into save something," she'd say.*

Isn't helping good, Gran?

"It is if you use your head. You've got so much heart, Maddie, sometimes it overrides your sense."

I shudder to think of what she'd say. *Oh Grandma, I wish you were here.*

I look up at the ceiling, knowing my tenant is above should I need help. Then again, she's deaf so how would she know I was in danger...

The man shifts and starts checking his pockets. Real fear skitters through me. "What are you looking for?"

"My phone," he rumbles. "We need help and..." He checks the last pocket. "Fuck."

"Should I go back outside and look?" I'm half thinking I should just leave. I know this is my house, but I've invited a strange man in, and my preservation instincts are kicking in.

I could always call for help. Where is my phone?

"No," he answers, his voice sharp. "If Vigo or Vincent come back, I wouldn't want you out there."

A little of my fear recedes at the way he is thinking of my protection too. Vincent does seem completely crazy. "Okay."

He lets out a long breath. "Fuck, my head hurts."

"Dizziness? Nausea?" I ask, moving a little closer, my hands clasped in front of me.

I'm still in that dress from my date, my hair spilling over one shoulder as I reach down to feel his head.

"Neither. Just a headache from where I cracked my head."

I nod, sitting next to him, tucking my hands under my legs. "So what do we do next?"

He rubs his head. "I just need to think for a second. I'm usually better at this but…"

But then, the sound of a distant car engine fills my ears. "Lights," I say, speaking clearly as all the lights dim at once.

The car grows louder and he touches my arm. "Smart."

I nod in his direction and then realize he probably can't see me either. "Benefit of not seeing so well. I've trained my ears and voice-activated most of the house."

His fingers skim down my arm, reminding me he's there, as the car revs up right in front of my house and then stops just in front. It sounds like Vincent's car, the one I just left.

"What should we do?"

But he's already pulling me to standing. Navigating around the couch, he crouches, tugging my hand with his. "We hide."

CHAPTER FOUR

MADDIE

BEFORE I EVEN HAVE MY bearings, I land in his lap.

He's sitting on the floor, his back to the couch, his arms around me as he presses me tight to his chest.

For the barest second, I forget that I'm afraid, forget that Vigo has come back to my apartment, and I just feel.

Because this man's body is the stuff of fantasy. Hard and lean it makes a girl…want.

I think back to my plans and hopes for the evening. Vigo is not a man I could trust my body with, but the man I'm touching...

His arms are wrapped around me, the hold so protective, his cologne and the slight scent of an oaked alcohol fill my nostrils.

I brace myself on his biceps, the muscles rippling under my hands. What would it feel like to kiss a man like this?

"Name's Roman, by the way." The deep smooth tenor of his voice pulls me deeper in, my brain completely losing every detail as he overwhelms my senses.

A loud banging on my door interrupts my carnal thoughts and I jump in Roman's arms. He holds me tighter.

"Shit," I mutter. "What do I do?"

His hands splay out on my back. "Shh," he softly whispers.

"Maddie," Vigo calls, rough and loud as he bangs again. "Open up."

"He knows I'm here," I whisper again, my hands climbing up to Roman's neck. The strong cords of it help calm my racing heart.

"He also knows you were in the doorway when his brother shot two people."

Excellent point.

"Maddie," Vigo bangs again. "You forgot your phone in Vinnie's car."

I gasp. Did I? I remember giving it to Kate. And then we got distracted by the car in front of my house. "Hide in my bedroom," I say to Roman as I start to pull up from his lap.

His hands slide to my waist, holding me in his lap. "Don't. It's better to ignore him. Vigo is not a man to underestimate."

I shake my head as I slowly push up. As far as Vigo knows, I believed him about the fireworks. He really could be here just to return my phone. "If I don't answer, he'll know I know."

With a low curse, Roman rises too and does as I ask, making his way down the narrow hall.

With trembling hands, I fully stand. "Coming," I say loud enough for Vigo to hear.

"About time," he rumbles. "I thought you might be deaf too."

Asshole.

I smooth my skirts as I make my way to the door, slowly turning the lock and then I open the door.

Vigo is standing on my top step, his arms crossed. Even his outline exudes the sort of power that has me shrinking back. I clear my throat. "Sorry it took me a minute. I had just undressed."

I hear him rumble his annoyance before he grabs my arm and pulls it toward him. I gasp out my surprise until the cold plastic of my phone case touches my palm.

I wrap my fingers around it and pull back, eager to get this over as quickly as possible.

But Vigo doesn't let go. In fact, he uses his grip on my wrist to pull me closer as he steps into my house. "Need help getting that dress back off?"

"I..." I swallow down a lump, the idea of his hands on me makes my skin crawl. "It's late and I'm really tired."

But he still holds my wrist in one hand, his other pressing my phone to my palm. His forearm is the only thing keeping our bodies apart as it presses against my right breast. "I dropped off Vincent and Kate."

He doesn't further explain as he starts pushing me backwards into the house as I try to make my brain work. "Vigo, if you want to go out again…"

"Nah," he says as he makes his way inside. "I'd rather just stay now."

I squeak out a protest. "Oh. But…" I plant my feet, which only means that Vigo's chest pushes against mine. He finally lets go of my phone to wrap his arm around my back. But that just means that my hand with my phone is trapped between our bodies.

"Hear any more fireworks?" he asks, as he slides the hand on my arm up over my shoulder to grasp my neck. His hold doesn't hurt but I'm not able to move…at all.

I'm trapped just like one of my broken animals, no place to go, completely unable to defend myself. "No. Why? Was it one of the casinos?"

The tension in his hand lessons and I let out a long breath. Did I lie convincingly enough that he'll leave?

"Not sure," he answers, and then he leans in, his lips so close to mine, I can feel the heat of his breath on my lips, and they curl in distaste.

I don't like his smell, it's wrong, and I turn my face to the side, still in his arms. That's what prey does when it's cornered. It freezes.

"Listen, Vigo, tonight was fun. But I…"

"You listen, Maddie," I can hear the way he's talking through gritted teeth. "I meant what I said about you being gorgeous. You're a looker. But you've also got something I want. Now…if you don't want to end up like Kate—"

"What?" The single word is out before I can hold back. "Where's Kate?" Fear washes over me and I jolt in his arms. He tightens his grip again.

"You're going to let me willingly into your bed, or better yet, I'm going to take you to mine, and then you're going to sign the papers I tell you to sign."

Roman was right. I shouldn't have answered the door.

I swallow down a lump, my heart roaring in my ears. I have no idea what happens next. I'm somehow between Roman and Vigo. Why do I ever leave the house? I should have watched that baseball game with Josh and Lucia.

If I ever see Lucia again, I'm going to tell her that I should have just stayed hidden. Tucked away. "I c-can't come with you. I have my animals to care for."

"I don't give a fuck about your animals." And then, before I can even react, he's bending down, wrapping an arm around my legs and lifting me in the air.

I scream, trying to squirm away, but it's as useless as a baby bird squawking. Until it isn't.

I feel the air moving a second before the sound of something hard hitting flesh fills the room.

Suddenly I'm falling to the side, my shoulder crashing into the hard floor. I cry out, curling in on myself.

A moment later a hand touches my other shoulder. I scream again, but gentle fingers grip me. "Maddie."

Roman's voice helps me draw in a breath and then another.

"Are you all right?" he asks.

I shake my head, trying to decide. "I think so."

"Come on, sweetheart, we have to go."

"Go?"

"Vigo's going to wake up very soon. I only knocked him out, bludgeoning a man to death in your house isn't going to play out well."

I start to sit up, testing my shoulder. "You want me to go with you? Just leave him lying in my living room?"

"That's right."

I shake my head, my hand still gripped around my phone. I've been rather stupid all night, but just this moment, I do what I should have done when I first found this man outside.

"Call nine-one-one," I say into the phone, which instantly dials.

"What are you doing?"

"Vigo is going to jail for attempted rape," I say. "I can't leave my home. I won't." Never mind that until Lucia forced me out last week, I'd barely left in months. This has been my home my entire life. I've never slept anywhere else. Even when I went to college…

Roman kneels over me, still calm but his body exudes power now. I look up at him, half in awe. "Sweetheart. Hang up. When Vigo doesn't return, Vincent is coming."

His words slice through me. Shit. He's right.

"Nine-one-one. What's your emergency?"

I only take one second to decide. I lift the phone to my ear. "I made a mistake. Butt dial. Sorry." And then I hang up.

He takes my hand and I let him pull me to standing and lead me outside. "I need to know where you're taking me."

I know I'm in deep trouble.

"My place," he answers. "I'll explain on the way."

I've made a few mistakes tonight that can't be undone. Can I trust Roman? Who knows.

But I can't stay here and wait for Vincent. I just heard him shoot two people. And I'd like to find a way to help Kate.

So that means I'm going with Roman. "My animals."

"I know a guy at a vet clinic. First thing in the morning, I'll have him come collect them. Promise."

He's already leading me out the door, his hand firmly around my waist. "Why? Why would you do that?"

"Maddie, if you hadn't brought me inside, I'd likely be dead."

That is another excellent point. For a guy with a head injury, he thinks clearly in a crisis.

He helps me into Vincent's running car and then closes the door. It takes him a few seconds before he comes around to the driver's side.

Is he all right to drive? But I don't have time to ask him before he's slamming the car into gear and squealing away.

He speeds through the Vegas night. I hear a rustling, like he's reaching into a pocket, before he speaks. "Call Mason."

I turn to him, my breath catching. Who is Mason and should I be frightened?

"Roman?" A voice comes through the phone.

"Mason. I need you. Now."

I'm about to find out.

CHAPTER FIVE

ROMAN

I SPEED THROUGH THE NIGHT, my head pounding as I listen to Maddie's frightened breaths.

Mason might kill me for not ending Vigo. The Vendettis are the kind of enemies you don't let slip through your fingers. Vigo shot at me just this morning. Vincent again tonight. In our war against the Italians, I could have made a major victory.

But I couldn't do it. Not in front of Maddie. I'm not scared of death, or of handing it out. My reason for hesitating is a long-game strategy.

I actually need this woman to trust me. Because in this war, the Vendettis pale in comparison to completing that tunnel.

I ignore the fact that she felt amazing in my lap. Or that I went absolutely insane when Vigo put his hands on her.

I don't do relationships, and certainly not with a woman like Maddie. One who requires extra attention and care.

I'm going to help Maddie now, make her feel warm and safe,

because she is the key, and if I'm careful, this whole night could play to my advantage.

Except for the part where I don't know where Luke is.

That scares the shit out of me.

As soon as I get this car into a safe location, I'm going to search the trunk.

I speed down the dark empty streets, probably doing eighty.

Fortunately for me, I've just moved from our previous Kincaid building and my new place is a property that no one in Vegas knows about.

Mason and I are careful to put some of our real estate through shell companies. It keeps our holdings from being known and it helps us in situations like this. I don't want to be found tonight.

I need to recover and then think. How am I going to deal with Vigo and Vincent? How am I going to use this interaction with Maddie to my advantage?

I've still got the phone to my ear and Mason is spitting a slurry of questions, but I can't talk and drive. My head is buzzing. Slowing down, I fumble with the button and finally hit the speaker function.

And then, I hand the phone to Maddie.

She feels it hit her arm and her fingers fumble to grab the device. "Hello," she breathes out, her voice trembling with fear. I wince, my fingers brushing down her arm before I grip the wheel again.

"Who is this?" Mason barks back.

"Umm. Maddie."

"Maddie?" Mason asks with all the disdain a CEO of a multi-billion-dollar company is capable of.

"Maddie Reid." Maddie croaks out into the waiting silence.

Mason pauses and I know he's beginning to understand. I will him to soften his approach but it takes every ounce of my energy to drive the car. "And you're with my brother, Roman?"

"Yes," she says, sounding scared out of her wits.

"Tell him what happened," I direct, punching the gas again.

In halting words, Maddie begins. "I was on a date with Vigo Vendetti and he was dropping me back home."

"You were on a date with Vigo?" Mason cuts her off. "Have you been seeing each other for a long time?"

This is what I appreciate about Mason. I'm normally good with details but tonight, I'm struggling. Between the head injury and my reaction to Maddie...

Mason is asking all the right questions. Maddie clears her throat. "This matters?"

"Yes," Mason says. "It does."

"No, first date."

"How did you meet?" he asks her, his voice softening. I can hear him closing doors in his house, moving about. Is he getting ready to leave? Come back to Vegas? I hope so. I could use some help right about now. Between Maddie and Luke, I need more hands.

"Bar. Last week. My friend convinced me to go out and he was there." She keeps going, telling him about the medical student who was out with Vincent. The return to her house. The two pops she heard.

"See anything?" Mason asks.

"She's vision impaired," I sigh out, finally turning into the parking garage of my building.

"Hear anything?" Mason asks without skipping a beat.

"I heard the trunk open and close," she answers. "After the...the shots."

I lean toward Maddie and the phone. "I'll check it as soon—"

"Don't." Mason talks to someone off the phone and then he's back. "I don't want your fingerprints anywhere near the trunk."

The word ricochets through me. He's assuming the worst. That Luke is dead.

My knuckles tighten on the steering wheel as I turn into the entrance for the parking garage. Slowing, I grab my phone from Maddie and hit another button to open the gate.

It clanks open and I pull through, shutting it behind me. As it closes, I let out some air. I stop the car and rest my head on the steering wheel. Fuck, my head is pounding.

"We need to see a doctor," Maddie is saying. How long has she been talking? I tuned out for a minute, but I hear her now. "I don't know how he drove, but I'm worried he has a concussion."

"Thank you, Maddie," Mason rumbles. "I have a friend that I can send to you for medical care so you don't need to leave the apartment again tonight."

"I offered for my friend Lucia to examine him. She's a vet, not a doctor, but Roman said..."

I lift my head and gently press the gas, pulling into a spot next to the elevator and slump down into my seat. Getting us here, took whatever bits of energy I had left. "You don't want your friend anywhere near your house," I say and then I close my eyes.

A small hand lightly touches my arm and then slides up my sleeve, skimming over my neck before delicate fingers twine into my hair. It's light and soothing but it infuses me with a bit of energy.

I have to get Maddie inside. She can't do it herself.

It's that thought that pushes me up out of the seat, opening the door, and stumbling around the car.

Her door opens too, and she steps out into the lights of the garage.

It's the first time I've really seen her tonight. She stands in a cute strappy dress that hugs every gorgeous curve, her long blonde hair flowing down her back.

Vigo's comment about her joining him in his bed is making a hell of a lot of sense.

Maddie is a knockout.

She keeps her hand on the frame of the car as she scoots around the door and I step up, placing a guiding hand at her waist, my arm curving around her.

Beautiful and so vulnerable.

She comes willingly into the cradle of my body, her breath catching. "I'm scared."

"I know, sweetheart." I tighten my arm which settles her even closer. Every instinct spurs me to protect this woman and my other arm comes around her, holding her close.

I've forgotten about Mason, forgot he's on the phone. "Get her up to the apartment," he orders. "You'll be safe there."

Mason's words help push me into action as I keep one arm around her, heading to the elevator.

The doors slide open, and I know as soon as we're inside, no one can touch us. This is the second building Mason and I built to be a fallout shelter.

They cost a fortune, but they'll withstand a massive earthquake or the blast of a bomb.

I hear another voice and I recognize the voice of my other brother, Leo. He and Mason are both married, and things have been so hot here in the city, they've taken their wives to our compound in Colorado.

"I'm coming too," I hear Leo grunt. Normally, I'd worry about Leo's temper. Right about now, however, I could use a bit of Leo's aggression. In fact, I think it might be exactly what this situation requires. I turn off the speaker and put the phone to my ear.

The less Maddie knows about my family, the better. Because as much as my head pounds, it's starting to work again. I don't think she realizes who I am. Doesn't know I'm the man who has been pressing her to sell her house.

Anonymity is a major asset.

"The women…" Mason starts.

"Will have the entire team of security," Leo answers. "At least for tonight, we're both going."

"We'll be there soon," Mason says as the elevator doors close. I know the call will cut off any second as I slump against the wall. "Take care of Maddie until I get there."

"Call Jack," Leo adds. "He'll bring the doctor."

The line clicks. After my father's death a few years after my mother's, Mason became my parental figure. Through my teen years, he was the man who sent me to college, who set me up with a job, who taught me how to hold a position of power.

We understand each other in ways most men would not. So I know his last words to me about taking care of Maddie were said for a reason. We both see the truth. She isn't just a small asset in this war, she's the key to the Italian's undoing.

I slide my fingers down her spine. I have always lived in Mason's shadow. But today…with Maddie…I might have finally made the decisive move that propels us forward.

"No sleeping." Maddie wraps her arms around me, squeezing. "I don't have a lot of experience with human medical care, but I know you can't fall asleep if you've got a concussion."

I lean against the wall, appreciating the feel of Maddie's body pressed to mine.

My hand settles into the small of her back, the curve perfect under my palm, as her full breasts crush to my chest.

Who knew Vigo and I would have something in common? I pocket my phone, my eyes closing, as I lift my other hand to her hair, running my palm down the silky length. "It was so dangerous to come outside and help me."

Am I chastising her for coming to my aid? The understanding of the danger she was in tonight settles like a weight on my chest, as I drop my nose to the crown of her hair. She smells like apple blossoms and crisp white wine.

It's such a strange mix for me. I'm feeling so protective over this woman, even knowing that if ever I was going to become emotionally involved, she is the last person, for several reasons, I should choose.

"My gran would have said the same," she mutters into my shoulder. "'No sense,' she'd say."

My hand on her back, fists into her dress. "Imagine if I was more like Vigo."

"You aren't?" she asks, shaking her head against my chest.

Is she worried she's not safe with me? I pick my head up, opening my eyes to study her. "I don't go around shooting people in the street." Except I do. I mean, not often. And in my defense, the man we killed today was attempting to kill us. Actually murdered my father in cold blood. Does that make me bad? Or the type of man who can keep the people around him safe?

Is it both?

And if I'm being honest, Maddie should be frightened of me. My intentions are less than noble.

Maddie doesn't pull away, if anything she burrows deeper into me, her face nuzzling into the crook of my neck. She breathes out, warm air rushing over my skin. "I just need to know," her voice has dropped to a whisper, "and I probably should have asked this before I got in the elevator, but am I going to be safe here with you? I don't know who you are or how you know Vigo."

My sweet little vulnerable bird needs to be safe, and she wants me to be her haven.

I can work with that.

Vigo unwittingly pushed Maddie right into my arms. He never was any good with the subtleties.

"To answer your question, I've known Vigo almost all my life. We grew up together, so I've got loads of experience with how shitty he can be."

She nods into my neck and then starts to back up. I feel the loss of her body heat and I let out the lowest rumble of dissent. I want her back on my body, her softness against me.

The elevator chimes and the doors slide open.

"Lights," I call out, the apartment lighting up. Everything in my apartment is voice- or phone-activated. It's part of the security that my Uncle Jake installed.

"You have voice commands too?" she asks.

"That's right," I answer, as I take her hand and lead her out of the elevator and into the foyer of the apartment. "What do you need me to do to help you navigate?"

"I can see enough," she answers, her fingers still twining in mine. "The lighting in here is good so I see the outline of things. Shapes. Blurs of color."

That makes it easier for sure.

My phone rings and I pause in the kitchen, Maddie stopping with me, as I pull the device out of my pocket and pick up. "Yeah?"

"It's Jack." Jack worked for my father before he started working for Mason. "I'm fifteen minutes out. I've got your doctor with me."

"Fifteen?" Good.

"Should I blindfold him?"

I see Maddie's eyes widen and, inwardly, I grimace. She can clearly hear Jack on the other end of the phone now that we're in the quiet of the apartment with no background noise. I want us both to be safe here. Which means keeping our location under wraps.

But I can see why blindfolding doctors might make her question the type of man she's with. She tries to pull her fingers from mine, but I hold tight.

"Can you put me on speaker?" I say to Jack.

"You're playing through the sound system. Dr. Levine can hear everything. Fire away."

"Dr. Levine," I say in my most polite voice. "Would you mind if Jack covered your eyes? We've had an incident with the Italians and we're trying to keep a secure location."

"Not a problem," the doctor answers. "Completely understand."

"Thank you."

I hang up the phone, pulling Maddie the rest of the way through the kitchen and into the living room to sit on the couch.

She follows my lead, but unlike the elevator, she doesn't settle against me as she sits, her fingers slipping from my grip.

"Everything all right?" I ask gently, leaning back and closing my eyes. My head is pounding to a steady thrum as I cover my eyes with my hands. I know how to soothe an upset woman. I've been trained since childhood.

"Fine. I..." She swallows. I uncover my eyes to see her hands twisted together in her lap. "I need some more information."

I reach for her hands again, covering them with mine. I feel her tremble of fear. "I'm going to protect you, Maddie."

She gives a little nod, but her body language couldn't speak any louder as she leans further away.

Is she worried? Scared of me?

She should be...

CHAPTER SIX

Maddie

The doctor comes and examines Roman. He doesn't have a concussion. I have no idea how to feel in this moment.

I've been like a pendulum, going back and forth. In some moments, I want to shelter in Roman's arms and then in others...I think I might have stepped into the lair of the beast.

A much more sophisticated predator than Vigo ever could be.

I sit silently, still on the couch as the doctor finishes. "And the lady?"

"I'm sorry?"

"Injuries?" the doctor asks in a gentle voice, his bedside manner like that of an office visit and not like he was blindfolded for a house call.

"She fell on her shoulder," Roman answers for me. "Left."

I am surprised he even remembers that happening. It was so crazy in that moment when Vigo dropped me. And honestly, the time in my living room when Vigo tried to carry me off feels like days ago, not just an hour before.

The doctor checks my arm, moving it this way and that, pokes the flesh, which is only mildly sore and declares me fine.

I'm not fine.

Remembering how Roman fought off Vigo helps me calm down, but I'm seriously debating asking the doctor for help getting out of here. Then Roman stands, placing himself between me and the doctor. He reaches into a pocket and pulls out a stack of bills, the slide of paper filling my ears as he counts out money and presses it into the palm of the doctor's hand.

I stand too, trying to see what numerical value is on them. Roman has excellent lighting but I still can't make them out, even squinting.

Are they fifty-dollar bills? One hundred? I don't know why this is important other than it adds to the feeling that I am way out of my depth. My weekly grocery allowance is less than a hundred dollars.

"Thank you," he murmurs just before Jack starts ushering the doctor back to the elevator.

I draw in a shaky breath, trying to calm my racing heart. I need to know some more details. Roman's last name might be a good place to start. Why Vincent shot him would also be helpful. But I'm completely at his mercy now and I don't know how much I can push.

Roman follows, whispering to Jack as they go. I can't make out the words and I rub a hand down my face, realizing that I'm bone-tired.

I'm never up past ten and it has to be three in the morning.

I sit back on the couch, contemplating the safety, or lack thereof, of falling asleep right here when Roman speaks, "Maddie."

His voice cuts through me and I sit back up. "I'm awake."

"You're fine, I just..." He comes to sit next to me, his arm coming around the back of the couch, his fingers brushing my hair as they pass. "You went very quiet."

"Just tired," I say, my chin dropping, as my internal debate rages.

I nip at my lip, trying to figure out how to proceed. Questions are swirling in my head. Swallowing down my reservations, I finally ask the biggest one. "What were you doing outside my house in the middle of the night?"

Roman stills. Technically, he hadn't been moving before, but his muscles get stiff, his breath slowing. "My cousin and I were out at one of the casinos. We just happened to stop in front of your house so that Luke could…"

I shake my head. Is he trying to tell me that Luke urinated on my wall? The casinos are only a few blocks away in either direction. It would not be the first time drunken partiers made a ruckus outside my house. Still… "The casinos? You don't smell like smoke."

Roman clears his throat. "VIP room."

His fingers gently brush my shoulder and I stiffen away. His voice only gets softer. "I know it was a bad idea to stop. Too many drinks and…"

It all sounds very reasonable but I can't quite dispel my fears. I came here because I couldn't stay at my house. I can't face Vigo or Vincent alone. But… "So you just happened to be wearing a bullet-proof vest and I happened to be out on a double date with guys who have the kind of beef with you that they'd try to shoot you?"

Silence meets my words. It stretches out between us, the tension growing with it. Am I on to something? Am I treading into dangerous territory? My arms wrap around my torso as I wait. Finally, he speaks… "Not completely."

"What does…"

The elevator dings and the doors slide open. My head jerks up, fear skittering down my spine. Who's here?

"Hey," Roman's voice is soft. Gentle. "It's all right. It's my brothers."

More men I don't know. I begin to tremble, I'm so in over my head. Maybe I should have just faced Vincent. I know who he is. I know what he planned. It was awful but it was right there in front of me.

Before I can articulate any of this, I'm scooped up by Roman. A small cry falls from my lips a moment before he settles me on his lap.

Roman's hands are gentle, as he slides down my arms. "Hush." His fingertips dance up my spine "No one here is going to hurt you."

I shake my head, the first tears of the evening pricking at my eyes. "This is crazy," I whisper.

"I know." His lips brush my temple, and I find my hand settling on his biceps as I press deeper into his lap. I'm frightened of him, so why does touching him soothe my fear?

"Roman," another man rumbles. I have no idea if it's Leo or Mason and I squeeze my eyes shut. I don't want to know.

"I'm fine. Maddie's good. Doctor just left."

"I know. We met him and Jack on the way out." This time, I recognize Mason's voice from the phone call earlier and I hear the way it drops low. Something is wrong.

I find my grip on Roman's arm tightening and he squeezes me, his hands splayed out on my back.

"Mason, Leo, this is Maddie." I turn to give them the briefest nod even as I bite my lip. Are there still tears on my cheeks? Most likely.

"Hello, Maddie," one of them answers. Likely Leo. It doesn't sound like the man I talked to on the phone.

"Hello." Why I feel the need to be polite, I don't know. My grandmother drilled it into me, I guess.

"Maddie's exhausted and frightened," Roman rumbles, the sound of his voice vibrating through my chest, before he clears his throat.

"I'm fine," I lie. I can't run, that's not an option for me. But I'm almost too tired to fake anything. Raw emotion is about to start pouring out of me.

"Why don't you go lie down." Roman's voice is honey and whisky, rich and deep with a touch of sweetness. "I'll only be a few minutes and then I can help you brush your teeth and change."

Is it a bad idea to leave them to talk? What will they plan for me? But it's a welcome thought to be in a room alone. I need to collect myself… "All right."

He stands, lifting me in his arms. Slowly, he lowers my feet to the floor, his arm wrapping about my waist.

I let him lead me down a dark hall and then I hear a door open as he ushers me into a room.

"Lights."

The room lights up and I can make out the bed in the center of the far wall. The room is large, the carpet thick under my feet. The bed looks heavenly, but I swear, I could curl up on the floor and sleep, I'm so tired.

Note to self, as attached to my house as I am, get tired enough and you can adjust to a new place.

He leads me to the bed and helps me sit. "Feel free to lay down, sweetheart. I will be right back."

And then he's gone. I do as he says. I lay back, my head settling on the pillow, and I close my eyes. Is that stupid? Maybe. But if these men want to hurt me, there isn't much I'm doing to stop it regardless.

I won't see it coming.

"Oh Maddie," I whisper to the room. "What have you done?"

CHAPTER SEVEN

ROMAN

I TURN ON THE SINK, running some water to mask our voices. "Keep your voices down. She's visioned impaired but her hearing seems to be excellent."

Mason raises his brows. "What secrets do we need to keep from her?"

I frown, disliking the words I'm about to say. But I'm searching for the advantages here. And I owe Mason solutions after all he's done for me. "As far as I can tell, she hasn't realized we're the Kincaids."

"Fuck," Leo rumbles.

But Mason only lifts his brows. "What does she think you and Luke were doing?"

"Pissing on her wall."

Mason scrubs a hand over his jaw as he considers my words. "And did you knock on her door after you were shot?"

"No, she came out when she heard me. She takes in wounded creatures…"

"Fuck," Leo repeats.

"It's an interesting opportunity," Mason scowls as Leo.

"The woman helped our brother," Leo spits, stepping up to Mason. "I can see the look in your eyes and I don't like it. Don't tell me you're going to screw her over."

"I'm going to find our cousin," Mason rumbles back, his shoulders pulling straighter.

"Don't start, either of you." I give both of them a push on the shoulder. Oil and water these two.

Mason recovers first. "Her tip was a good one. Hearing the trunk."

That makes me focus. Did Mason discover something that will help us locate Luke? "You find anything?"

"Yeah…" Mason winces. "Blood."

"Fuck." It's what I was afraid of.

"Any chance Luke had a weapon on him?" Leo asks.

I shake my head. "No. We just went there to look at the size of the property that had been flagged by the inspector. Try to figure out why Maddie is so resistant to sell. We didn't think anyone…"

Leo lets out a frustrated rumble. He's right. It was stupid and reckless.

Mason glares at me. I get it. I'm supposed to know better. Do better. Mason would never make a mistake like that. "So Luke was loaded into the trunk of the Vendetti's car with no weapon, after being shot."

"That's about the gist of it."

"Was he wearing a vest like you?" Mason is going through all the details now.

"Yes." That makes me feel slightly better, despite knowing there was blood. "And Maddie mentioned the other woman, Kate, is in med school, I think."

That gets both my brother's attention. "That is good." Leo's anger is forgotten. "Really good."

"Did Maddie like this girl? Is there any chance they exchanged numbers?"

I scrub at my jaw. "It's possible. But how to find out…"

"Jake can definitely get the information, but we'd need her phone." Mason's brows lift.

"Jake just left Vegas."

"He's got to come back," Mason says with a shrug. "This is a situation that requires everyone."

I figured as much. But I'm delaying answering Mason's request for Maddie's phone. She's so vulnerable being dragged here. Without a phone, she'd be even more so. Completely dependent on me and even more suspicious. Then again, this is Luke's life. "That's for sure."

"The phone, Roman." Mason directs us back to his request. "Can you discreetly collect it?"

"Why don't we just ask her for the phone." Leo scowls at both of us.

"I don't want her to know who we are yet," Mason rumbles. "I need time to make a solid plan. If we can get her land, we win. Game fucking over."

I know he's right. It's what I've been thinking all night.

"How long do you think you can keep it from her, Roman?" Mason asks, giving me that look that slays me. Like he's almost, but not quite sure, I'm worthy.

My shoulders tense up. "I don't know. She's wondering why Vincent would shoot us to begin with. Why I'm wearing a bulletproof vest. She must already suspect we're in something dark and dangerous."

"I say tell her the truth," Leo holds up a finger. "You were there to look at the land you wanted to buy. You're a legit businessman, but Vigo is not."

I frown at my brother. Leo's gone soft since he got married. Still, the plan holds a certain appeal. If I'm honest, I don't want to go at Maddie hard. She deserves my cloak of protection, not more deception.

Then again, Mason has excellent instincts. He's led us this far. If he thinks that we should keep Maddie in the dark, maybe he's right.

"I think it's a long shot she'd give us the phone. She's already nervous."

"I agree," Mason nods. "Right now, you're the man she rescued, who is now rescuing her back?"

"What did Vigo try to do to her?" Leo asks, his arms crossing over his massive chest.

That makes me shake my head as I remember Vigo hauling her up on his shoulder. I had this moment where instinct took over and every cell in my body was intent upon protecting her. On making Vigo pay for even touching her. "He tried to kidnap her. He specifically mentioned his bed and then paperwork."

"The Vendettis have the subtly of charging rhinos." Mason grits between clenched teeth. "But if Vigo mentioned paperwork, it wasn't an accident he was out with Maddie, he was making a move against us."

Neither Leo nor I speak. Because Mason is one hundred percent right on this one. No argument required.

"And we can't discredit the possibility that Maddie might be in league with them."

Those words hit me like a punch to the chest. Sweet, innocent Maddie? A deep part of me does not want to believe it. But Mason's instincts are better than mine. And there are a great many coincidences tonight…

"Just give me twenty minutes and I'll get the phone." And with that, I turn off the water.

Mason reaches up a hand, to hold me a moment longer. "Gain her trust, Roman."

Leo scoffs. "You're never going to get it lying. Even I fucking know that. I know you two are sympatico, but I'm telling you, you're doing this wrong."

"He's been married a week, and now he knows everything about women," Mason fires back.

I leave them to their argument and start out of the kitchen and down the hall. I've already made up my mind.

I enter the room to find Maddie sound asleep on my bed.

For a moment, I just look at her. Her face is so innocent, her blonde hair streaming out over my pillow.

Her hands are folded on her stomach, her perfect tits peeking out from the top of her dress, her long legs on full display.

I reach out and touch her cheek, the velvet of her skin sliding under the rougher pad of my thumb.

Her eyes blink open, her brow creasing as she stares in my direction. Does she not know who I am? "It's me, Maddie. Roman. I thought you'd want to brush your teeth."

"Roman?"

I reach for her hand and brush my thumb over the back of hers. I've always been good with the particulars of caring for people. Especially women. Their clothes, their products. I can look at a woman, know her size. See her skin and understand which tones would complement her.

I spent my childhood helping my mother hide her alcohol abuse. Cleaning her up, painting her face. I know how to do care…

"That's right. It's me." I pull her up from the bed. "Want to wash your face and put on something more comfortable for sleeping?"

I let go and she wobbles on her feet.

Not bothering to pretend she should go on her own, I sweep her into my arms and carry her into the bathroom.

Reaching into a drawer, I pull out a carefully packaged satchel with a new hairbrush, toothbrush, and basic necessities like deodorant, shampoo, and conditioner. I keep them for the female guests I occasionally have stay.

I say occasionally, because I frequently don't like the complication of even casual relationships.

"You just have all these things ready to go?" She fingers the small bag.

I chuckle. "I like to be prepared." Then I pull out the toothbrush and apply toothpaste, handing it to her. She starts to brush her teeth, and I leave the bathroom to fetch her a T-shirt.

Coming back in, I grab her free hand, placing the shirt in her open palm. She takes it and lifts it to her nose. "It smells like you."

Another person who loves the details. "Does it?"

"You're very good at this," she holds the shirt close to her face. "Taking care of me. You do this often?"

I laugh off her words. "Not often. I'm just organized. What about you? How often do you have male guests?"

"I've never had one."

I stare at her, all the laughter gone. Some deep ache settles in the pit of my stomach, tightening my balls. "But you said that you've never slept away from home."

"I haven't."

I suck in a breath, realizing the truth. She's a virgin.

I just got done saying how I don't like taking care of women. I don't. But Maddie has been pulling at something deep all night.

I watch a blush stain her cheeks as she turns back to the sink. "I've got it from here. Thank you."

But I don't go. Instead, I touch her hand, the heat of her skin practically searing me. She's a virgin. A complete innocent. It pulls at me like a moth to a flame. I don't even know why. It's not something I've ever even considered, never articulated I wanted. But it makes her even more...special. Unique. Mine...

Her chin is tucked, her cheeks the sort of pink that makes me want to kiss every inch of her. I cannot afford to catch any kind of feelings now.

I've got a plan and she is just one tiny piece. I can't let that thought go. She is a means to an end.

She washes her face, the water glistening on her pale skin. Silently, I hand her a towel, our fingers brush, making me clench even tighter.

"Roman?" she turns to face me, her skin glowing after she's washed it.

"Yeah?"

"Can you undo my zipper?" she points to her back.

Slowly, I grab the metal tab, pulling the zipper down as more and more of her skin is exposed. I could kiss a trail along that skin, drink in her taste. Instead, I turn toward the door and give her a moment of privacy to take her dress off and put my T-shirt on.

"I'm ready," she calls when she's done. I enter the bathroom again and take a moment to drink in the sight of her in my shirt. It's like I've left my mark on her. Claimed her. My chest tightens, but I force myself forward.

Gently, I lead her to the bed. She settles in and I tuck the covers around her, "Dim the lights."

The room darkens and she curls on her side, asleep in seconds.

"Good night, Maddie Reid. I'll be back in to check on you in a bit."

She lifts her head. "Where will you sleep?"

"On the couch."

She lays back down, but I feel her hesitation. The way she tenses. "Is it weird if I say, I don't want to be alone?"

"No. Not weird at all. I'll let you fall asleep and then I'll join you. Don't worry. I know how to stay on my side of the bed."

With a nod, she closes her eyes, rolling over to turn away from me. I give it a moment. Two.

Reaching for her phone on the nightstand, I slide it into my waiting palm and leave the room.

CHAPTER EIGHT

Maddie

I wake slowly, warm and comfortable. I can't remember the last time I slept so soundly, and I try to discern why as I stretch.

Only, I don't. Stretch.

Which is when I realize that my legs are tangled up with someone else's and the reason I'm so warm is that I am snug against a hard body.

I jolt awake, pushing up, when an arm I didn't even notice was around me tightens. "Morning, sweetheart."

Roman's hand spreads out on my hip, my bare hip, as I realize the T-shirt I'm wearing is up around my ribs.

I pull my head back, enough sun filtering in that I can make out the lean edge of his jaw and his muscular chest.

His naked chest. My hand comes down on it to create some distance, but I freeze, the feel of his muscles incredibly hot. My fingers dig into his skin, loving the rougher harder planes of his body.

"Why are we in bed together?"

"You asked me, remember?" he answers, stretching as he somehow still holds me firm against him.

"I forgot," I whisper, my hand splaying out on his chest to push off of him. Only I pause because, holy crap, what a chest.

"You needed to be warm and safe, sweetheart, after everything last night."

"I…" That's all I get out before, with a flick of his arm, I'm on top of him.

My other hand comes to his chest too, but I'm not even trying to push away. Instead, I double down on the massage I'm giving his pecs.

I have no idea why I'm behaving like this. Last night, I barely trusted this man. But everything seems nicer in the light of day, and this is a moment I've waited for…for forever.

I don't have to see Roman to know he's gorgeous. I can sense it in his movements. Hear it in his voice. He exudes the sort of confidence that shouts handsome alpha male.

He wraps both his hands around my thighs, parting my legs and settling my knees on either side of him.

He's wearing boxers, but they're thin material and even with my panties, I can feel the long press of his…umm…guy parts…exactly where I need it most, and I let out a small moaning gasp, rolling my hips.

Is it crazy how primed I am? How good he feels with almost no ramp up?

He slides his hands up the back of my legs to grab my ass and then I'm pressed even deeper into him, the pressure so good, I grind into him and toss my head back.

His hands are so strong as they bite into my hips, helping my body move with his. I take my palms from his chest and lean back, placing them on his thighs instead to change the angle.

It's even better and the throbbing ache intensifies as he lets out a rumbling growl. "Maddie."

My name in that rough voice, unlocks something inside me and I bite at my lip as I slide over him. "That feels so good." But I know I want more. I want to hear him say my name like that again. I want to feel his hands everywhere.

This is what I envisioned when I said I was ready to lose my virginity. This is the promise I've spent years picturing alone in my bed.

Scared as I was to leave my house last night, I think I've been ready to grow. Feel and experience.

"You like that, sweetheart?" he growls out, letting go of one of my hips to run his hand over my waist and ribs before he cups my breast, brushing the nipple with the pad of his thumb before giving the whole thing a squeeze.

I've always been well-endowed in the chest. I fill his hand and he gives my soft flesh a squeeze as I gasp out my pleasure. At the same time, he makes this low, guttural sound deep in his throat.

My hips are moving faster, it's like I'm possessed as the tension inside me grows so taut I think I might break.

I arc into his hand, wanting more of him. All of him.

That's when his phone rings on the nightstand.

It makes me stutter and I start to lift away when he holds me in place. "Ignore it."

And then he works my hip with his hand, sliding me along the long hard length of him. It's all I need to do exactly what he's commanded. I ignore the phone as we keep going at a more leisurely pace, which is a sweet torture all of its own.

The phone finally stops, which is my cue to ratchet up the pace. Roman's body under mine is like nothing I've experienced before and I want more.

But then the phone starts ringing again.

He stills me with his hand on my hip as he lets go of my breast, pulling his hand out of my shirt. His shirt, actually. Reaching over to the nightstand, he glances at the phone. "It's no one."

He flicks it on silent and then holds my hips again, our bodies grinding together. It's everything I dreamed it would be and I'm mindless as I chase the pleasure he so effortlessly gives.

I'm pretty sure I'd walk through hell just to make sure he kept touching me.

CHAPTER NINE

ROMAN

I PUSH her panties to the side, my finger sliding through her soaking-wet folds. "Christ," I grunt at how good she feels. How wet she is for me.

This was not the plan. I started the night on the very edge of the bed. I honestly meant to just comfort her. Gain her trust. For all I know, Mason is right. She was planted by the Italians and is here to learn our secrets...

But when I woke up with all that silky skin on mine, all my reservations evaporated.

She makes this squeaking noise as she pushes down against the friction I'm giving her, her body so arched, her tits are staring at the ceiling.

I reach her entrance and push inside, sinking deep into her pussy. "You're so tight," I groan, pushing in even deeper. I want to feel more of her. See more. "Take off my shirt."

A minute ago, she was playing shy. Not now. Straightening, she grabs the hem and tugs it over her head, nothing but her pushed-to-the-side panties blocking my view of her as she straddles my hips.

Holy fucking Christ.

I've seen beautiful women before. But Maddie. She's absolutely perfect.

High, full tits, tiny waist, flat stomach, and the flare of her hips… she could make a man beg.

Lucky for me, though, she's the one who moans out… "Please. Roman, please, I need…"

"I know what you need." And then I sit up.

My arm locks like a vise around her back as I curl my back far enough to pop one of her sweet nipples into my mouth, sucking on the pale pink flesh as it puckers in my mouth, her pussy rippling around my finger.

"Yes," she cries out, arching again in a way that shoves her nipple deeper between my lips, I suck harder and press the heel of my palm into her clit as I pump even deeper inside her.

She's going to cum very soon and I can't wait to hear her, to feel it. I can't remember the last time I was this amped for another person to orgasm.

I could lie and say this is all tactical.

But I know the truth. Maddie is like catnip and I'm a fucking tomcat. She's so beautiful and vulnerable and…

She lets out this keening moan that wipes my brain clean, her pussy so tight around me as I switch to the other nipple, running the flat of my tongue over her before I suck that one into my mouth too.

It unravels the last of her control and burying her fingers into my hair, she pulls with both fists as she screams out my name, breaking apart on my hand.

Maddie is soft in nearly every way, but fucking hell, she makes all the best noises when she cums.

She grazes the lump on my skull which hurts like hell, but I ignore it. The pain is worth the experience.

I'd love nothing more than to bury myself deep inside her, but I know she's a virgin, I can feel how unused to this kind of play she is, and I don't want to hurt or scare her.

I can't lose my head. And honestly, I know it's a problem, but my feelings are not just tactical. I want her to feel good.

So, using my arm that's around her, I flip us both so that she's on her back with me above her.

Keeping my finger inside her, because I love how she feels, I pull my other arm out from under her and pull my cock out from my boxers. I give it a few quick tugs. The idea of my cum on her belly has me rumbling with need. "Maddie, I'm going to—"

She doesn't say anything but one of her small pale hands lifts up, the tip of her finger brushing over the head of my cock.

My teeth clench together. How can the skin of her finger be that soft? She does it again, using her thumb to rub right on the opening and I start to leak cum, the visual of her touching me making me even hotter.

She collects the liquid on her thumb and then licks it off, her facial expression growing thoughtful. "Salty."

"Maddie." It's a half plea, a part command. My balls are boiling with cum.

Who fucking knew Maddie would be such a willing and incredible bedmate?

I'm so fucking amped up, a few fucking pumps from my own hand and I'm ready to explode.

"I've always wanted to know how it would taste," she whispers as she reaches for me again. But this time, her delicate fingers are brushing mine away, before they wrap around my cock, which looks ridiculously large in her small hand. "Show me how," she says, propping up on her other elbow.

Without a word, I wrap my hand over hers, helping her pump my cock in her small fist.

She gasps, just a small sound as she adjusts her grip based on the pressure from my fingers.

She's so responsive to my every subtle direction, every shift of a finger that thirty seconds in, I can already feel my balls tingle, the cum moving up my shaft, as our hands work together.

Together…

It adds this layer of intimacy that I can hardly process. I don't do feelings with the women I sleep with.

But Maddie, she's blurring some line as she licks her lips. "I don't wish this very often anymore, but this once, I wish I could see all of you. Like really see you, not just the blurry outline. I bet you're beautiful."

I blink back my haze of lust. Beautiful is hardly the word for a man about to cum. My cock is an angry red with veins popping. "My little bird, I'm a raging beast." I even sound like an animal, the words grunted out as I try to remain focused.

She nips at her lip, working her hand even faster. "A beast? I've always wanted one of those."

Something in her words triggers my orgasm. I want to be her beast. I want to fucking devour her.

But also…for the first time in my adult life, I want to keep her safe too. I roar as the cum shoots from my cock, splashing across her belly. It goes on and on, my body spasming until I finally wilt on top of her, my stomach pressing to her cum-covered belly, my lips finding hers.

The kiss isn't sweet, it doesn't coax, it claims. Which is ridiculous. A few hours ago, I promised to lie, cheat, or steal this woman out of her home. For all I know, Mason is right and she's an agent of the enemy, here to seduce me and not the other way around.

She is the one who asked me to share the bed.

I shouldn't want to claim her.

Then again, I just might be the man who is able to have his cake and eat it too.

Speaking of, I want to know how she tastes.

And I am not talking about her mouth.

I kiss down her jaw and over the tender flesh of her neck, even as she turns for me, exposing more of her sweet skin. I'd like to kiss every inch of her on my way to my final destination when I look over to see my phone is still ringing. Fuck. How long has it been going off?

I don't want to jump up to answer. First. I like holding Maddie. It's an oddity for me, but even after the orgasm, she feels so good, her skin sliding against mine. If anything, I don't feel satiated.

I want more.

But I need to pick up the phone. This could be about Luke.

"I'm sorry, sweetheart," I murmur as I kiss her neck and reach for the phone, as I reluctantly climb from the bed.

"Hello?" I'm walking away when the voice on the other end of the line stops me in my tracks.

A voice I don't recognize rages in my ear, "What the fuck, man?"

CHAPTER TEN

Maddie

"Who the fuck is this?" Roman barks into his phone.

The hard tone of his voice stops me first. It's a side of Roman I haven't seen. Should I be scared?

I hear an indistinct male voice coming through the speaker piece of the iPhone. He turns around and comes back to the bed, holding out his phone as he presses a button. "Maddie, you need to hear this."

"What is it?" I ask, a different fear fluttering in my chest. What does this call have to do with me?

"Is this Miss Reid?" The caller asks.

"Yes."

"I'm from the LV Veterinary School and Clinic. We've been asked to take over the care of your animals."

"Yes?"

"There is a Lucia Anderson here who is demanding confirmation that you wish us to remove the animals from the premises. She's been blocking the removal for the last forty-five minutes."

My mouth drops open. Lucia is there? It's a Sunday and she is usually at the clinic Monday and Thursday afternoons to help me out unless there is an emergency. "Put her on the phone, please."

Roman mutters something under his breath but it's blocked by the grumbling of the tech. "Now I need to hand over my phone? What a train wreck."

Finally, Lucia's voice rushes through my ears. "Maddie?" she asks, sounding breathless.

"You didn't have to grab my phone like that," the man rumbles in the background.

I swear I hear Lucia make a face at him. "Hey," I gush, so glad to hear her voice. Much as I didn't want the moment with Roman disturbed, it's way better I talk with her. It grounds me and makes this whole thing seem way more…normal. "It's me."

"It is you!" She sounds relieved a moment before she follows up with. "What the actual fuck?"

I smile despite myself. "It was the longest, weirdest night of my life."

"Maddie?" And this time she sounds scared.

"I'm all right," I answer. "And I can't wait to tell you what's happened. You said I needed a bit of excitement, and I'll have to remind you of that again before I tell you everything, but right now, the vet school should take the birds and squirrels, I'm not going to be home for…" I cock my head in Roman's direction.

"A little while," he whispers close to my ear.

"A little while."

"You never leave your house. What the hell?"

"Like I said. It's a long story."

"I tried to call you like twenty times," Lucia demands, not letting it go. "Did your phone die or something?"

I twist around, reaching for the nightstand but my phone isn't there. All I feel is the hard wood surface. "Oh. I don't know…I thought I had it."

"Maddie, I was about to call the police when you didn't pick up. That's when I came here and found these people removing your rescues. I've been freaking out."

Roman's hand covers mine, giving them a squeeze. I swallow. "Roman," I start. "Can you give Lucia your number so she can call your phone direct if she needs to contact me? Just until I find my phone."

"Who is Roman?" Lucia's voice is growing louder with every sentence.

But before I can answer, the line clicks. Roman starts to set the phone down, but I shake my head. "Don't bother. Lucia—"

The phone rings.

Roman just hands it to me.

I take it, squinting to see the answer button. It's light enough, if I really try.

"Sorry, sweetheart," he mutters and then clicks the button himself.

But I cringe. Just when I was feeling like a normal girl…

"Hey…"

"Hey yourself," Lucia bites back. She is the most wonderful person, and an amazing friend, but laidback is not her vibe. She's an ass-kicker.

"Don't be mad."

"I'm not mad. Just confused. And scared. And…"

"Vigo turned out to be the second biggest asshole on the planet." I've got to short-circuit this conversation.

"Who's the biggest?" she asks, her voice getting much softer, and I know she knows she messed up pushing me to go out with him.

"His brother, Vincent. Who was on the date with us."

"Shit."

"I can't even begin to tell you what a nightmare it was, but the long and short of it is Vigo is a criminal and a murderer."

"Maddie! You're not serious."

"I couldn't see, but I could hear and—"

"Wait. You're not saying you saw him murder someone?"

"I don't know if Luke is dead or not, but I heard the pops."

"I'm confused. Who is Luke? Where are you now? Who are you with?"

I sigh. "Yeah. Like I said, it's a really long story. But Roman is the guy who rescued me from Vigo."

She's silent on the other end of the line for a second, two, three. "Lucia?"

"I mean…" I hear her draw in a deep breath, "you're not with Roman Kincaid are you?"

I start, my entire body jolting with the reaction as my head snaps up.

"Maddie," Roman whispers as I drop his phone, scurrying away. How could I be so stupid?

That is why he was outside my house, he lied to me.

He wants my property and now he's got me all but trapped in his apartment. Wherever the hell that is…

I keep sliding back, doing some reverse crab crawl as I try to escape.

But I'm not used to the contours of the bed, and I'm not really judging my surroundings. Where I think there is going to be bed, there is air, and suddenly I'm falling.

I let out a scream, even as strong arms wrap around me, pulling me against a hard chest.

"I've got you, sweetheart," Roman rumbles, holding my almost-naked body against his. My instinct is to throw my arms around him as I try to anchor myself. Which is so fucked up.

"Are you okay?" Lucia cries, her voice filling the room from where I dropped the phone on the bed.

"I'm fine," I answer, my whole voice trembling. "Roman caught me."

"Where are you? I'll come get you," Lucia sounds as panicked as I feel, and I unlace my fingers from around Roman's neck to scramble for the phone again. I want to keep her on the line. If I lose Lucia now, I don't know, I'm somehow worried I might never find my way back.

"Lucia," Roman calls, not moving despite my frantic searching. "Last night Vincent Vendetti shot my cousin and tried to shoot me, all while Maddie was a witness."

"Witness? She's fucking blind."

"It's not safe for her to go back to her house, nor is it safe for her to be at yours if the Vendettis know who you are."

"Shit," I gasp out. "Is Lucia in danger?"

"I should have never made you go out with him," Lucia cries. "I'm so sorry, Maddie."

"Lucia," Roman soothes. "I need to be clear. If you think your safety is at risk, I need you to call me. I can have you stay here. We have plenty of open apartments where you would be safe."

Some part of me unwinds. Did Roman just offer to bring Lucia here? To have her live in this building? My body stills, relaxes. It's exactly what I needed to hear.

"Vigo doesn't even know my last name," Lucia huffs.

"Good," Roman reaches for my arm then, gently pulling me toward him until my chest is against his once again. Then he wraps an arm about me, keeping me in his arms. "Stay away from Maddie's place. Call this number whenever you need to until we find her phone. Call me if you need me to come get you."

"Okay," Lucia sounds as confused as I feel.

"I promise I'll keep Maddie safe."

"Okay," Lucia says again, but she doesn't sound certain. Which is weird because Lucia is always certain.

Roman hangs up the phone before I've even said goodbye, his arm still around me.

"You're Roman Kincaid?" I thump his chest lightly with my hand. I've never been more unsure in my life. Is Roman what he seems to be or have I run from one beast straight into the arms of another?

CHAPTER ELEVEN

MADDIE

"I AM."

"Why didn't you tell me?" I hear the hurt lacing my voice. I just let this man touch me in ways no one has before. What little I thought I knew about him has been colored and I don't know how to see him.

"Maddie," he whispers and then he leans in to kiss me. I feel it coming and turn my head to the side so his lips land on my cheek. This conversation would be so much easier if I weren't still mostly naked and pressed against his bare chest. "Try to understand."

"I don't. Not at all."

His other hand settles just above the curve of my ass, his hand spreading out in a possessive hold that steals my breath. "Your date took my cousin."

The air whooshes from my lungs. Because. Yeah. "I…"

"Imagine if it was Lucia," he says and my stomach twists into knots.

"I…"

"It was an oversight on my part. I was not thinking clearly, I had a head injury, but I never lied to you. I introduced you to my brothers. I took you to my home. Do I seem like a man trying to hide truths from you?"

My arm wraps around his neck then, my fingers gliding over his hairline as I bite my lip. "No."

He gives me a squeeze, though I swear I feel tension move through his muscles like a wave, down his body. "All right then."

I swallow down a lump. "Thank you for catching me."

He drops his forehead to mine, our breath mingling. "I'd never let you fall, Maddie."

No tension this time, I feel the truth of the words right down to my bones. I'm melting into him then. Part of me still worries that I shouldn't, but he offered to let Lucia live here. He caught me when I could have hurt myself, he...

He made me feel things no one has ever made me feel before. His mouth finds mine, and this time I don't turn away. He gives me a soft, warm kiss that lingers and teases. It's full of promise and, dare I say, affection, and it's more than I ever imagined a kiss could be.

I have this thought that I could just give myself over to this man and damn the consequences. Whatever price I pay later will be worth the pleasure now.

His hands trace my hips, giving me a light squeeze at my waist and then skim up my ribs, his thumbs caressing the sides of my breasts.

I love the feel of him. His skin, the long length of his body, his large strong hands. I could drown in his touch.

He slides his hands up to my shoulders, down my arms and then over my back. Dipping lower, his palms caress the back of my legs before cupping my ass and pulling my hips into the cradle of his.

His tongue tangles with mine as the kiss goes on and on. I'm breathless with want as I wind my fingers into his hair, my body so open to him, I'm practically begging for more.

That's when his phone rings. Again.

He doesn't stop, the kiss lingering, but I feel the change as he slowly retracts, his body less molded to mine.

All too soon, he picks up his head, one of his hands leaving my body to grab the phone again. "Hello?"

I force myself not to sigh.

"Hey," a male voice responds.

I don't get this many calls in a month. Then again, maybe that's a me problem.

"Jack. Hang on one second, Maddie's about to get in the shower."

Was I? I'm pretty certain I was being kissed like no woman ever has before. But Roman's forearm wraps under my behind, lifting me with one arm, as he carries me to the bathroom.

"I can call back," I hear Jack say into the line. "It's Maddie I actually need to speak with."

"Why's that?" Roman asks, stopping.

I cock my head too, curious why Jack would wish to speak with me. "I found this cat…"

I give a small cry. "Is the cat injured?"

Roman puts the phone on speaker.

"I don't know. I think so. He was lethargic behind one of the tires of my car when I came out this morning."

"Where is the cat now?"

"In my car. I didn't know what else to do."

I'm tapping Roman's shoulder. "We'll need cat food. A crate. A litter box." I keep ticking off the list of supplies, my fingers drumming against his skin.

"Why would we need cat food and a litter box?" Roman asks sounding mildly frightened. "Jack can take the cat to the vet hospital. They'll—"

But I'm frowning as I tap him again. Having something to care for, that would make this situation so much…easier. Normal. It's what I do. I take in wounded creatures and I heal them. Or I try. Give them the life they might not have had if I hadn't intervened.

"Can I just examine the cat? Please?"

"I'll be over in twenty," Jack says before Roman can answer.

I hop down from his arm, and reach my hand for the door, only needing to feel for the knob twice. I'm getting the hang of this place already. "Can you show me which bottle is the shampoo and which is the conditioner?" I say, making my way into the bathroom. "And how to turn the shower on."

"Of course," he says, following behind me. "Or...I could just help you wash your hair."

I turn back to him, wrinkling my nose. "I can wash my own hair."

"I know," he answers, pulling me close. "But wouldn't it be more fun if I helped?"

Heat infuses my cheeks as our bodies crush together again. I have got to get some clothes on, because every time my skin slides against his, I forget all my reservations and worries.

Which is how Roman ends up in the shower, peeling my underwear off right along with his. I can't believe it. I'm completely naked with a man.

And not just any man.

Roman is the most of everything. Masculine. Rich. Powerful. It's intoxicating and dangerous, and as he soaps up every inch of my body, I know I want more of him. Just like I know I shouldn't.

His lips find mine again and we're back to those kisses. The ones that feel like hugs and sex all at the same time. Sweet and intimate and yet they make me breathless with want.

By the time he's washing my hair, I'm ready to beg him to take my virginity. Who needs it anyway?

That' s when the damn phone rings again. I know mine is currently missing. And his phone is my one connection to Lucia. But I'm ready to toss that thing out the nearest window.

My body is humming again, the need to orgasm pulsing through me, even though I came like a half an hour ago, and I just want Roman all to myself.

"I'm guessing Jack is here."

"Twenty minutes goes by quickly," I murmur against his lips. "In the shower."

He chuckles, low and deep. Intimate.

And then he helps me out, wrapping me in the fluffiest towel I've ever felt. The only thing I have to wear is my dress from my date.

Roman helps me into it, zipping up the back. "We'll get you more clothes today."

How will he do that? Will he go back to my place?

The elevator door dings, and Roman leads me out into the living room.

"Shit," I hear Jack curse a moment before the scamper of paws on the hardwood sounds through the apartment.

"Where's the cat?" Roman asks, his hand tightening around mine. "Jack? Where is the cat?"

"Ah, behind the couch, I think."

I give a small laugh. That is very much what a cat would do. Because I live where I work, I don't have cats or dogs. Too much risk with all the small animals who are my patients. But I'd love to have both.

My grandmother had, or likely still has, me on a list for a Seeing Eye dog. But the wait is endlessly long, and I've never pushed because of what I do for work.

It's another reminder of how I've not moved forward in any metric for a long time.

"What's our kitty look like?"

"Black and white. Big. Fierce-looking eyes."

"Maybe a male then. If he's large." Letting go of Roman's hand, I move to the couch and bend down slowly, making sure I'm not going to bump anything. "Did he go behind or under?"

"Under," Jack answers.

Dropping to my knees, I press my face to the floor. "Hi there," I croon, only to be met with a hissing growl.

"Oh. I see," I say to the cat. "You're not sure you're ready to be friends."

Sitting up, I call to Roman. "Got any tuna?"

"I do."

A minute later, I put a small chunk just under the couch. Quick as a flash, a tiny paw darts out and the tuna is gone.

With a small laugh, I give the cat another piece. Then I sit up again. "We'll get the cat out from under here, but it might take a bit."

Jack rumbles a sound of regret. "Sorry, Roman. Should I wait?"

Roman shakes his head with a sigh. "No. The cat will stay until we can get him out from under the couch."

I hear Jack mutter. Is he relieved? Regretting rescuing the cat? I'm not. Giving the cat another chunk of tuna, I call over my shoulder to Jack. "What's wrong with the cat again?"

Jack clears his throat. "Seemed lethargic. It was just hanging out next to my car."

"Hmm. Cat isn't lethargic now. Then again, this is a new, scary environment."

Neither man answers as I push up. "I'll get some water. We ought to set up a litter box after all, just to save your floors."

"Litter box?" Roman asks. "How long is the cat going to be under my couch?"

I shake my head. "Might be a few days. He'll come out when he thinks it's safe, but it might take us some time to build up enough trust to get him to come out in our company."

I hear Roman sigh. "I'll pick up a few supplies while I get your clothes."

"Thank you, Roman," I breathe knowing that the cat will give me something to focus on. Dropping to my knees again, I softly call to the cat, who does not come out but has stopped hissing. "Before you go," I speak softly, still down on the floor. "Can we pull out the bed to see if my phone is behind it? That's the only place I can think of."

"Maybe you left it in Vigo's car when we drove here?" He asks, the tenor of his voice changing again. "Like you did on your date?"

"No. I know I had it in the bathroom," I answer and then I make a few kissing noises at the kitty. "If I can get the cat out and find my phone I can send a few pics to Lucia."

"Use mine," he answers quickly. "It's no trouble. Since Jack is here, I'm going to have him help me pick up clothes and supplies, but I'll only be gone a few hours. You can call me on his phone if you need me."

Then he walks toward the kitchen. "Let me leave you a plate of food before I go. You should eat."

I nod my thanks, completely intent upon the cat. While Roman is gone, I can compile a list of logical questions that help me better understand him and this crazy situation. But for the moment, it does me good to focus on the furball under the sofa. Something that has nothing to do with anything.

Or so I assume.

CHAPTER TWELVE

Roman

I head down the elevator and find Mason waiting in a Honda Civic. He slides out of the passenger's seat and climbs into the back, Jack taking the driver's seat. Driving Mason is one of Jack's regular jobs when Mason is in Vegas.

Mason is about six feet tall, and I'm closer to six-one, making the back seat of an economy car a tight fit. His feet fill the entire space behind the driver's seat.

"Interesting choice," I say as I climb into the rear passenger's seat and shut the door with a resounding thunk. I've never felt more like a sardine in a tin can.

"Looks like a Civic, outfitted like a tank," he answers.

"Bulletproof glass and everything," Jack adds as he backs out of the parking spot.

That's when I notice the rips on the seat in front of me. "Apparently the upholstery isn't quite so sturdy."

Mason grimaces. "I had this car made to look as economic as possible. It's like a cloaking device of sorts."

"You couldn't have picked an Accord? They've got a lot more room."

Mason ignores me. "And had it fortified so that if we didn't blend into the crowd, we'd still be safe." He turns to me then, glaring. "What I never planned for, was having to chauffeur the meanest cat in all of Christendom."

"That's Jack's fault," I point at our long-time employee and friend. "He picked the cat."

"This was all your idea. That vet tech picked the cat. And he seemed pissed after this morning, so I should have known he'd give us a mean one," Jack fired back, before shaking his head. "But I have to admit, it worked like a charm. She's completely focused on the cat."

My shoulders sink down as the gate opens and we slide into Las Vegas traffic. "Thank you. I'm going to need every distraction I can get. She figured out that I'm a Kincaid."

"Already? How'd she do that?" Mason asks, his irritation clear.

"The tech is pissed because when he went to pick up the birds, Maddie's best friend Lucia, a vet, showed up and demanded to know why the animals were being removed from a state-sanctioned sanctuary. And when Lucia tried to call Maddie and couldn't get through…"

"Shit," Mason rumbles.

"Yeah. By the time the phone rang through on my end, panic had ensued."

"That doesn't explain how she found out," Jack points out.

"Lucia realized the moment that Maddie shared my first name," I glare back. "Smart as a whip and super sassy, that woman."

Mason grimaces. "It's unfortunate, but it can't be helped. She'll be more suspicious of any overtures you make toward the property now, though. Don't bring up the sale if you can help it. Not until we've got a solid strategy."

I nod. "Fine." But I'm starting to hate all these lies and half-truths. From omitting my last name, to manufacturing a cat in need, I'm playing on her sympathies and distracting her while we search her phone and attempt to abscond with her home.

And get Luke back.

We pull into a back alley, a salesclerk already waiting with a large clothing bag dangling from her hand.

"I've taken the liberty of having all the goods you need for Maddie assembled for us. We'll hardly step out of the car."

"That's usually my job."

Mason gives me a smile. "I have an eye for detail too, little brother. And Maddie was easy. I just said she looked like Marilyn Monroe. Lots of chest, tiny waist, nice ass—"

"Mason." I cut him off, the growl in my voice a clear indicator of where I stand. His eyes narrow in response.

Jack pulls up and gets out of the car, taking the bag and placing it in the trunk before returning to the car. "Pet store?"

"Yes." I scrub my face. "I'll call them now."

I call a boutique shop that assures me they'll have a care package together in the next half hour. When I hang up, I stare at the phone, feeling like shit about the choices I've made today.

"How much did that cost you?" Mason asks with a chuckle.

"Who knows," I shake my head.

Jack snorts from the front. "Like you care about the cost. What you should be worried about is how many distractions it's going to take. What's next? A parrot?"

I drop my hands. "Hopefully not."

"What then?" Mason asks, lifting a brow.

"He's seducing her," Jack answers for me.

I frown. For some reason, I don't like talking about what Maddie and I are doing behind closed doors. It's never bothered me before. I mean, I don't go out of my way to share sexual conquests, but it doesn't irritate me. Not usually. Not like today. My fingers clench into a fist.

This is not information I want Mason to have.

"Already?" Mason leans back, giving me a long stare.

I shrug. "The opportunity was there. I took it." The words sit bitter on my tongue.

But Mason doesn't look pleased. "Be careful with that one."

"If you're thinking that she's somehow going to take advantage, you don't need to worry."

"I told you last night, her connection with Vigo makes her a suspect," he answers. "And Maddie's got that deadly combination of beauty and innocence that can trap a man, if he's not careful. If they wanted to plant a spy, they couldn't have chosen better."

It's totally true. "A blind spy," I grunt. But I know his theory has merit. Still, she seemed legitimately shocked by my identity this morning. "You didn't see her this morning. She freaked out when she found out who I was. She'd have to be a first-rate actress."

"Just be careful."

I nod my agreement. Spy or no, Maddie needs a strong man to look after her. And me, I'm nearly as strong as they come. "If you think I'm going to catch feelings, you needn't worry. Mom cured me of any need I have to look after a needy woman."

"Mom?"

I shake my head. "It doesn't matter. I'm not going to fall in love, if that's what you're afraid of."

"I sometimes forget how much more you were with her at the end. Leo and I were both off already. But you had to watch—"

I cut him off. "You don't think I have the stomach for this."

"Maybe. Maybe not."

I glare at him. Much as Mason has been like a father, he frequently questions my ability to get a job done. I am forever proving myself.

"I won't hate myself when the Vendettis are in jail, or when Luke is returned, or the tunnel makes us impenetrable." I use the words to fortify my own thoughts.

Mason grimaces as he faces forward again. "Good. So we stick with the plan. You distract her, keep her at your place, win her affection, and find a way to purchase that property."

We arrive at the pet store, an employee already walking out with a large bag in one hand and a crate in the other.

Jack gets out and gets the goods, placing them in the trunk with the clothes. The door slams as he gets back in.

I give him a questioning stare, wondering what all that is about. But he only glares at me in the rearview.

I glare back. "What?"

"Didn't your Uncle Jake teach you not to trifle with beautiful young women? They should not be used as pawns in this war."

I let out a rumbling breath. "Who asked you?"

"I'm not your lackey," he spits back. "I speak when I want." Then he glares at Mason even harder. "You, of all people, should know better."

"She holds the key to a fifty-million-dollar construction project that will give us dominance over all of Vegas and end the Italians once and for all."

Jack harrumphs. "Crushing an innocent, handicapped woman because she's in your way? How are you any different from the Italians?"

Mason curses a string of words, each more foul than the last, sounding furious.

"Luke's life—" I start.

"Luke is a grown-ass man who's been handy with a gun since the age of ten," Jack spits back. "Taught him myself. But Maddie..." And then he stops, shaking his head. "You make sure whatever you take from her, you give back tenfold. You hear me?"

I do. Loud and clear. And the truth of Jack's words sit like a lead ball in my gut.

The rest of the ride back to my new apartment is silent, until we turn onto my street. Then Mason turns to me. "Stay out of sight from here on out. I have no idea how hot this is going to get, but your job is to stay put, keep Maddie safe, and keep the construction project going."

"I know," I say, Jack's words still knocking around my head.

"And as for Luke," Mason glares at Jack. "The Andrianis didn't have any luck discerning if Luke was at the Vendetti property or not, and considering the hostile takeover they're about to engage in on our behalf, it seemed best not to push. But they did give us the Vendetti's address. Leo is going to lead the raid himself."

"When?"

"Tonight."

"I want to be there."

"No," Mason shakes his head. "You have your job."

My jaw clenches. In some ways, Luke was more of a brother to me than my actual brothers. We grew up in the same house, after my dad died, my aunt taking me in. "Fuck that. Luke needs—"

"Luke needs you to shut down the Italians."

My jaw clenches, my teeth grinding together, but I don't argue.

We arrive at my apartment building and pull into the garage. I get out, collecting the bags from the trunk before I head up the elevator.

I grimace as I think on Jack's words. He's the second man to tell me I'm taking the wrong path when it comes to Maddie. When Charlotte, Mason's wife, landed on Mason's door, I was the one advocating that Mason do right by Charlotte. It seemed so simple when it was Mason.

The floors tick by until I reach the penthouse, the doors sliding open again.

I don't need to call out to Maddie, the moment I step into the apartment, I see her stretched out on the couch, sound asleep.

What's more, the cat is curled up on her belly.

Matted and vicious looking, the little devil makes a low noise in the back of his throat the moment he spots me, but he doesn't get up. Doesn't retreat.

No. Instead, he narrows his yellow eyes and lets out a hiss.

"So you think you're the Tom, do you?" I say in response. "I think if you're going to stay, you need to know, that I'm the alpha around here."

The hissing turns into a singing growl. He's definitely telling me to fuck off in cat language. There is no doubt.

I cross over to Maddie and lift my hand to push him off her belly when, quick as a snake, he lifts a paw and rakes his claws over my hand, leaving deep scratches. "Fuck."

Maddie wakes with a start, her hand settling on the cat, who immediately starts to purr.

"Roman."

Her eyes flutter closed again. "Sorry. I must have fallen asleep. Last night was…"

"I know," I bend down again, only for the cat's purring to turn into hissing once again. So that's how it's going to be, is it?

Does this cat not like men?

Or can it sense that I'm planning to coerce and betray his loving benefactor?

CHAPTER THIRTEEN

Maddie

The cat does not like Roman.

I hide a smile. Cats can be like that. Selective in their allegiances. But in this case, Roman has opened his home to both of us and I need this kitty to make friends.

Especially because everyone assumed this cat was a boy… It's not. It's a girl, and I'm nearly certain she's pregnant.

There are going to be baby kittens very soon. Not that I'm telling Roman that quite yet. I don't want him dropping the cat on the nearest corner. Having the cat here makes me feel way more…

At home.

I give Roman a sleepy smile as he holds up two bags. "One for each of my guests."

"Oh, thank you," I murmur as I gently move the cat, who does not seem pleased to be shooed off my lap.

"Tom has taken to you, I see." Roman sets down both bags and opens one.

"Tom?"

"The cat," he answers. "He's out from under the couch already."

"The quiet helped," I say, bending down, the smell of kitty litter hitting my nose as Roman pours it into the litter box.

He slides it on the other side of the couch and then reaches in and pulls out several cans of what I'm sure is cat food, and a bowl.

Tom lets out a loud meow. I give a little laugh.

"How much do I give him?"

"Half a can and one scoop of the dry," I answer. Lucia has a cat, so I've got some points of reference. I'm glad Roman's completing the task, though. It will help them bond.

Roman fixes the food but before he can even set the bowl on the floor, Tom is up on the counter, eating while Roman still fills the bowl. "Well, I guess keeping cats off the counters…"

"It's not really a thing. Do you mind?"

"It's fine," he answers. "Now, for your bag."

"Did you go to my place?" I ask moving toward him.

"No. I went to a store. Or more specifically, I went to a shop that will bring a bag out to my car. They specialize in comfortable yet stylish lounge wear. But I asked them to add a few dresses, just because you look amazing in that one."

I feel my cheeks heat.

The truth is, clothes are one more area I'm not great in handling. Lucia buys most of my stuff since my grandmother died. My gran did it before that.

But thanks to Lucia, I've got cute hip-hugging jeans, and lots of soft cotton fitted shirts. Roman takes my hand and leads me to the bedroom.

I'm reminded in this moment that I'm not even wearing underwear. Mine were soaked this morning, and I'm not talking about the shower.

"Sit," he commands as he leads me to the bed.

Then he begins pulling items out of the bag, handing them to me.

Soft tops, silky underwear, lacy bras slide across my hands. "Roman…" I have no idea how much he spent on all of this, but I can feel the quality.

He stops. "If you're worried about the cost, don't be."

"Of course I'm worried about the cost." I've never even had a boyfriend. People don't just give me gifts. I'm holding a very soft sweater in my hands, the fabric so smooth as I crinkle it in my tightening fingers. It feels wrong to take gifts from this man. I can't quite put my finger on why.

He steps closer to me, his fingers dancing along my jaw. "Maddie, it's the least I can do. I've upended your whole life."

"Technically, Vigo upended my whole life," I whisper back. Now that man should buy me a whole new wardrobe. Not that I'd ever accept a gift from him.

Roman's fingers slide around my neck and into my hair as he cradles my head in his very large hand. "That is very true."

I give my throat a delicate clear. "I compiled a list of questions while you were gone."

His fingers stiffen against my scalp. "What kind of questions?"

My throat tightens as a I take a deep breath. This is the man whose body was plastered to mine this morning. Asking him for a few details shouldn't be weird. Except we don't really know each other.

He drops into a squat, his face now below mine. "My name is Roman Kincaid. I am one of five owners of Kincaid Enterprises, worth billions of dollars. Our primary business is Las Vegas real estate. Apartment buildings, casinos, clubs. Our current project is to build a tunnel underneath Las Vegas, a feat of engineering that doesn't disturb the skyscrapers above, while connecting several of our properties and the properties of some of our preferred associates."

I blink in surprise, digesting these words. They make the picture a lot clearer. "Am I to assume that the tunnel does not connect to any of Vigo's casinos?"

"It does not."

My shoulders slump because Roman does not sound like a criminal. But he's being hunted by one.

"And the offers on my house. Who made them? You?"

"Luke."

"And why does he want it?"

Roman hesitates. "We need to vent the tunnel."

"So the tunnel goes under my house?"

"That's right."

"And if I don't sell?"

His hand slides down my arm until he's grasping my fingers in his large hand. "Luke was in charge of the construction project, so I don't have the details."

My head pulls back. Luke, the man who was kidnapped. It makes so much sense. But in terms of Roman, it's also very convenient that he's not the man with the answers I seek. "What are you in charge of?"

"I run the casinos."

My eyes close, my fingers still held in his. "Did you bring me here to convince me to sell?"

"That's Luke's department."

"But you run the casinos. Your business is dependent on that tunnel."

He doesn't answer and I turn my head away, my eyes still closed. He's not brought up the fact that his family has made several offers on my house, but my time alone, with a cat purring on my lap, brought some clarity.

Vigo mentioned me signing papers when he threatened to carry me off. "Vigo asked me out because of my house, didn't he?"

"I couldn't say."

"If you were to guess?"

"I'd guess that you are correct."

"Did you bring me here to convince me to buy my house?"

"I brought you here because your life was in danger. And because you saved mine."

I want to believe him. I really do.

I draw in a deep breath of air, letting it out slowly. "My grandmother died last year."

"I'm sorry for your loss."

I shake my head. I wasn't asking for sympathy. "I dropped out of college the year before to take care of her."

"She was sick?"

"Dementia," I softly whisper. The memories are still painful. Watching the strongest woman I know slip away was an experience that's left deep wounds. "She raised me after my mom left."

"Your mom left?" his voice is so soft, but I can still hear the pain in it.

"I'm a lot," is all I answer. Who wants to fully share that she ditched out when she realized her daughter was blind.

His fingers lace through mine. "And your dad?"

"Never in the picture." I shake my head. "The only person who stuck by me is my grandmother."

"And that's her house."

I nod. "I grew up there. It's been my home my entire life, and every nook and cranny reminds me of her."

"That's why you won't sell."

I shrug, knowing how much I've revealed. But I've held back too. Because there are things that Roman can only know when I trust him. Things that would allow him to take my house right out from under me. And that house is not just my tether to the world, it is my world. "I hope you understand."

"I do. Perfectly."

CHAPTER FOURTEEN

ROMAN

THE REST of the evening is quiet.

I make Maddie dinner, helping her to the stool at the counter where we eat.

I can't help but compare Maddie with my mother. Maddie is the first woman to live in the same space with me since my mother's death.

And while Maddie is not a drunk, there are certain similarities. I had to feed my mother too. It's where I learned to cook. She'd need me to cook for her to sop up the alcohol.

It touches some deep chord. This is the exact kind of relationship I've been carefully avoiding.

Any woman is too much commitment for me. But Maddie would be this other level…

Not that I'm not tempted.

I sit next to her, glancing over as she delicately eats, her blonde hair tumbling down her back.

Sick fuck that I am, there's a part of me that wants to brush it out. Run my hands through it, as I carefully style the silky strands. For some reason, when it comes to Maddie, I'm turning into a masochist.

I clear my throat, sitting back on my backed stool. "Tonight, I'll let you have the bed."

She looks over at me, and I catch the slight wince. Does she want me in the bed with her? Trust me, I want to be there.

While I'm feeling conflicted about the relationship, I'm crystal clear on the sexual energy sparking between us.

I want Maddie more than I've ever wanted any other woman, and I intend to have her.

But not tonight. I've got business and she's not ready.

"Where will you sleep?"

"On the couch," I answer, setting down my fork.

I need to leave and search Luke's office, but I'd prefer Maddie not know I was gone at all. I wish I was going with Leo to look for Luke myself. But I trust Mason.

Or I usually trust Mason. Today tested that trust. Between banning me from Luke's search and throwing shade at Maddie…

But I'll hold the line. Mason is our fearless leader.

She takes another bite of the chicken and tahini sauce that I've made, her jaw softly chewing until she gives the meat a delicate swallow.

I silently make her a few promises.

I'll make certain her future is secure.

I'll see that she has a facility, a place to live.

I know it won't be her grandmother's house, but I can install all the latest features, make it as comfortable a place to live as it can possibly be. No stairs, voice-activated everything, proper lighting.

Maddie deserves that.

She deserves a great deal more…

I grimace as I pick up my fork again. I still hate taking her grandmother's place away.

"Everything all right?"

"Fine," I answer.

"You know..." She twirls her fork on her plate. "You don't have to sleep on the couch. I..."

Is she inviting me into the bed with her? My body hardens at the thought of having her pressed against me. Her curves molded to me in the best way last night.

But I've got another agenda. "I need to work late anyway. I've got financials to review, and rosters to look over."

She gives a quick nod. "Of course."

I get up from the counter, taking my plate to the sink and loading it in the dishwasher. "I can take yours whenever you're ready."

She nods. "Given a bit of time in your place, I can do these things myself. I do at home."

I wince, knowing I'm trying to take that home away from her. But honestly, she'll adjust to a new place.

Still, the thought has me opening the fridge. "Would you like a glass of wine? I've got a beautiful white open that I brought back from Italy."

"No thank you," she replies, getting up with her plate. With one hand on the counter, she walks around the peninsula.

She reaches me and I take the plate from her hand, loading it into the dishwasher. She reaches down too, her hand gently tracing several edges. My cock swells. I want her hands on me like that.

The way her fingers softly explore, trailing, tracing...it's sexy as hell.

"You're sure you don't want wine?" I pull down a glass for myself.

She shrugs. "Can I try just a sip of yours? I'm not much of a drinker."

I stop, watching her as she finishes exploring the door of the dishwasher and straightens. "No alcohol for you?"

She shakes her head. "I'm impaired enough."

My chest tightens. How does this woman always manage to slip past my defenses? I set the bottle down next to the glass and reach for her hand.

Maneuvering her around the dishwasher door, I pull her into my arms. She molds to me, her torso pressed from shoulder to hip against me, her arms winding around my neck.

Did I say I was going to wait? Take things slow?

I'd like to pull her into the bedroom right now, kiss every inch of her, watch her hands on my body.

Her face burrows into my neck, her nose sliding along my skin.

The wine is forgotten as I lift her up, carrying her toward the bedroom.

"I can walk, you know," she says, sounding a bit breathless.

"I like carrying you," I answer. The strange part is that I do. Taking care of her is feeling less like a burden and more like…

I stop in the middle of the bedroom. I can't follow this thought. Because maybe I feel like that now, but how will I feel a year from now? Two?

I don't do this. I don't have relationships.

Her fingers slide in my hair, skimming around the lump that's still there from last night. "How's your head?"

"Much better than yesterday," I answer, closing my eyes to feel the skimming of her fingers over my scalp.

"And your chest?"

There is a very dull ache where the bullet punched into the vest. "A small bruise. That's it."

"Any news on Luke?"

My heart rate increases, blood rushing in my ears. "Not yet." I drop my forehead to hers. "I know you're worried about Kate. As soon as I know anything…"

"Thank you."

I start moving again, making my way into the bathroom, Maddie in my arms. It's not even eight but the sun has set, and I really do have a great deal of work to do before I go to sleep.

Maddie brushes her teeth in one sink, me in the other. She starts to wash her face and I head back into the bedroom, pulling out a cute pajama set for her. Shorts and a tank.

It's the right blue to match her eyes.

Returning to the bathroom, I find her brushing out the long strands of her blonde hair.

Not able to help myself, I reach for the brush, gently removing it from her hand before I start to brush the strands myself. "Your hair is so healthy," I murmur.

"Most men do not notice those particulars," she laughs back. "But maybe because I can't see the strands, the feel of them is super important to me. I can't abide split ends."

I gather her hair in my hand and kiss her neck. I'm back to being that masochist. I told myself I didn't want this kind of relationship, and I don't. So why do I feel so satisfied taking care of her? "I laid out your pajamas."

She looks over her shoulder. "Roman."

I can hear the disapproval in her voice. "How are you going to find all these things on your own while you're here?"

"Help me learn. Okay?"

"Okay." I take her hand then, slowly leading her back toward the bedroom. "How much can you see?"

"The lighting in your apartment is excellent so I can see the broad shapes. I just don't make out details."

I nod. "See the dresser right in front of you?"

"Yes."

"Your clothes are in the top two drawers."

She nods but her steps slow. "Is there any room in the closet?"

"Yes." My stuff only takes up half the massive walk-in.

"Can I hang a few things? It's easier for me to identify items when they're on hangers."

"Of course. We'll move anything you'd like tomorrow. But for tonight," and then I pull her toward the bed, "let me help you into the set I picked out."

She shakes her head as she lets me turn her toward the bed. "I can..."

"I'm sure you can dress and undress yourself," I rumble. Putting clothes on her isn't something I'm gray about. This is a job I just like doing, no reservations.

My hands on her skin is just fucking fantastic. "Now come here and let me take off your clothes."

CHAPTER FIFTEEN

Roman

"I'm coming to pick you up," Mason says by way of introduction when I pick up the phone.

"For?"

"We've got to go to Kincaid Enterprises tonight."

I take a moment to consider. "You think it's a good idea to leave Maddie alone?"

"If we're going to move the tunnel project forward, we need to look over all the documentation that's in Luke's office."

I let out a long sigh. "That makes sense. You're right. It's just... wouldn't you rather wait until morning?"

"No. Not really. I'd rather be there alone when we can search without answering to anyone."

He's got a point. Not that employees will be rude, but they will wonder why I'm hunting all through Luke's office when he's out. It will stir a whole lot of questions. "You don't need to come Mason."

"Why don't you want me to come? Are you meeting up with Leo?" His tone is demanding, accusatory.

"No. But I am trying to complete the job you gave me, while leaving you to do yours." I look at the pile of shit on my desk, the stuff I planned on working on tonight. I understand why Maddie won't sell. How am I going to convince her? And if I can't, is there another way?

Because the idea of taking her house is a job I hate more with each passing hour. The feel of Maddie's skin under my hands as I took off her clothes and slipped on the pajamas, still lingers at the front of my thoughts.

She's softer than silk, her curves are fucking killer… And then there was the smell of her arousal.

It still lingers in my nose from when I helped her pull on those little shorts. Bent down, not only could I smell her, but if I'd just tipped forward…

"Right," Mason lets out a long breath of air into the phone. "Look. If we search tonight, first thing tomorrow morning, we can start calling inspectors, city officials. But I think we need to know the vague outlines first."

"Fine. Come get me." I pull the phone away from my ear, glaring at the phone. "And for the record, I was never meeting up with Leo tonight, though I still think I should be with him trying to get Luke back."

"We're soldiers," he grunts. "We do the job we're told."

I stand from my desk, my hand clenching into a fist, my knuckles turning white.

I've always followed Mason. He's been like my father when my own detonated. But right now, today, this… "The job has never been this dangerous or this fucking shitty." My knuckles rap on the desk. "I've got to ask. Is it worth it?"

I sit back down, scrubbing a hand down my face, but I'm not done. "I know the Italians started this war when they killed Dad. But he was fucking a boss's wife. Are we going to lose Luke avenging Dad? Hurt Maddie?"

"What about Mom? She suffered too."

My teeth grind together. Mason is wrong. That doesn't belong at the Italians' door. "Their marriage was shit. She was home with three boys while he was off fucking and fighting his way through Las Vegas."

"You're right, Roman," Mason agrees. "Dad should have been protecting her. Instead, he abandoned her to a pile of shit. She deserved better."

Anger boils up inside me. "Maybe. But she turned around and shoved that pile of shit right on me."

Mason is silent. "What was it like at the end?"

"She barely fed herself, didn't shower, didn't do a thing but sit in the fucking dark and—" My teeth gnash together, cutting off my words. "She didn't take care of me or Arabella. Did you know I walked our sister to school every day?"

"Roman," Mason says, his voice tight. "I wish I'd been there."

"You were away at school. Why would you have been home?" I stand, starting to pace the office. I've said too much. Maddie is stirring a storm inside me and I don't know what to do with all these feelings I thought I'd buried deep.

"Yeah, but you were what? Ten? You needed real support."

"I'm strong now," I say, waving his words away. "Mom made me strong. I'll say that."

Mason pauses before he slowly speaks. "Is Maddie being there a problem? Should she come stay with me?"

"No." The word flies from my mouth with far more aggression than I intended. As much as Maddie is pushing some buttons inside my head, we're on some course together and I can't steer away.

The very idea of her being under Mason's protection makes me want to break things. "She stays here."

"And you're still going to make sure she sells?"

"Yeah," I say, but my voice lacks conviction. "What's the alternative? Abandoning the project?"

"Which I know you know can't happen. We're almost to the end of this game."

I shake my head, staring at the wall. "The costs are fucking mounting."

"Listen. I'll be there in twenty minutes. We'll go to Luke's office and we can talk more in the car."

"All right." I hang up and spend the next five minutes standing in the middle of my office, considering all of Mason's words.

Then, I make my way into my bedroom.

Maddie is on the far side of the bed, curled on her side. Only a sheet covers her body and I can see the clear outline of her frame, the generous curve of her hip, the river of blonde hair snaking over my pillow.

I could just climb into the bed, shape myself around her, wrap her in a cocoon of protection and forget the world.

I've got more money than I could spend in a lifetime. We've been fighting some war and it's time to ask the question.... Is it worth it?

Mason didn't want to hear it tonight, but I'm still asking it.

She sighs in her sleep, soft and high, the sweet note of it rippling over my skin. Fucking hell, what this woman does to me. She's got me rock-hard with a single noise.

I turn away, scrubbing my face and head for the door.

I don't use the elevator, I don't want to wake her.

Instead, I take the stairs, using the time to consider what I'll do if we find Luke. Or...if we never find him.

I stand in the parking garage, listening to the night as the traffic of Vegas whizzes by. We're close enough to the strip that I can hear the people, the nightly party has begun. It makes me tired.

The Civic pulls into the garage and Jack gets out, signaling for me to drive. I'm glad I skipped the wine as I slide into the driver's seat. "Thanks for driving. I'm two scotches in," Mason shrugs.

"You're not usually a mid-week drinker."

"I miss my fucking wife," Mason growls, not even bothering to disguise how much he loves Charlotte.

"Is that why you're in such a rush to see this all done?" I back the car out, leaving Jack in the garage. I get that Mason's whole world is Charlotte now. But I won't hurt Maddie simply so my brother can leave Vegas.

"Don't make it sound like that. I'm in a hurry to move the tunnel along to help Luke."

That's fair, and I feel like an ass for even saying it. "I'm sorry. I know you're looking out for Luke. And I don't blame you for missing your wife. What's it like, loving someone like that?"

"Charlotte is my whole life. Our relationship is way more fulfilling than any deal I've ever closed."

I shake my head. "But taking care of her, it doesn't...weigh you down?"

Mason looks over at me. "No. The thing about the right relationship is it gives as much, if not more, than it takes."

I consider those words as we make the short trip to Kincaid Enterprises. Silently, we take the elevator up to the penthouse and we make our way through the conference rooms to the offices.

Stupid fucking Luke. I told him not to go to Maddie's house. If he'd listened...

I make my way into his office, the top of the desk an absolute mess. "How does he get anything done like this?"

Mason crosses to the shelf of liquor, pouring himself another drink. "You two are quite the pair. Never a thing out of place with you and with him..." Mason waves at the desk.

"We both know Aunt Gina raised me after Mom died. Luke and I shared a room. It was hell and it was great."

Luke was a mess and Aunt Gina would come in and clean it up so that I didn't have to live in his filth.

But it goes deeper than just being a mess. Luke struggles with numbers and letters. A fact he hides from everyone, even Mason. Is that why he nearly missed a deadline? I should have helped him more...

Mason takes a seat in the extra chair in the corner as I search through Luke's piles. If you can call them that.

There's no rhyme or reason to them. and after fifteen minutes I start systematizing. Papers from the building inspector, plans from the architect, random paperwork from the city.

Which is how I find a sheet that makes the blood freeze in my veins.

Maddie's address is at the top and as I scan down the page, my eyes close for the briefest second.

There are several years worth of back taxes that are owed on the property and there is a lien from the city because of them.

I look at the dates and I know, as her grandmother got sick, she lost the ability to make the payments.

There have been several recent payments, an attempt to remove the lien but it's not gone.

"Mason," I draw in a shaky breath. "Do nonprofits have to pay taxes in the state of Nevada?"

"Depends," Mason answers. "Why?"

I set down the paper. "What about someone who is legally blind?" Mason went to law school and now develops real estate. These are easy questions for him to answer.

"No. Someone who is blind should be exempt. Again. Why?"

I sit down in Luke's chair, a heavy breath falling from my lips. "The city has a lien on Maddie's property."

Mason instantly understands the full weight of my words. One, we could take the property in a second because of that lien. We'd have the city foreclose and then snatch up the property in foreclosure. Mason has the connections to expedite the entire process. But two…the lien is unfair. Maddie has been a full-time resident of that property her entire life and should be exempt. The taxes should never have been owed in the first place.

"Fuck me," Mason mutters and then takes another long swallow. "What do you want to do?"

I shake my head. "I'll file for the extension for the permits tomorrow. That buys me time." And then, I don't know.

I'd be the worst sort of asshole if I took that place from her. I'm not even buying it from her, knowing she should be able to keep it.

"Let's get Luke back first," I say, my voice barely above a whisper. "With any luck, Leo will find him tonight."

Mason gives me a long stare and I know he wants to push. He doesn't.

Instead, Mason and I leave again, going back to my apartment, barely exchanging a word. I make my way up the stairs and into the kitchen. The couch is all made up, and I shrug off my shirt, my pants, stripping down into nothing but boxer briefs.

But instead of laying down, I make my way into the bedroom. Is it wrong to watch her sleep? I don't know.

I reach the edge of the bed and stop. Maddie has shifted, she's now flat on her back in the middle of the bed, one arm tossed above her head.

The tank top has ridden up, revealing the smooth expanse of her belly, her tits so plump and round, I want to bury my face in them.

Her eyes flutter open. "Roman?"

"It's me," I say, my voice hoarse. "I couldn't sleep."

She scoots over, lifting a hand to beckon me into the bed. "Come."

I don't hesitate, climbing in next to her, wrapping my arm around her back to settle her body against mine. Her face nuzzles into my shoulder, her leg settling over my thigh, tangling between both of mine, as her arm rests over my chest.

She feels so fucking good and all the noise in my head quiets into one single thought.

This night has only just begun.

CHAPTER SIXTEEN

MADDIE

I MEANT the invitation as a comfort, a way to help Roman fall asleep. But the moment our bodies tangle together, I know.

This embrace is neither quiet nor soft. Energy crackles between us as his hand slides from the small of my back to the spot just above my ass.

I tilt my face toward his, knowing what I want.

Yesterday, everything felt out of control. Crazy.

Today, I'm caring for a cat, I know who Roman is and I think I know his agenda. And I know mine too.

I've been dying to be in bed with a man who makes me feel like Roman.

And here I am…

Is it the best of circumstances? No. Will I have this opportunity again? Who knows. Am I justifying? Absolutely.

But when his hand slides back up to my waist and then dips under the elastic of the little shorts I'm wearing, I don't protest.

In fact, I shift my leg so that I'm spread wider as skims his hand over the crack of my ass and then dips his fingers between my legs.

Liquid fire spreads through me as my back arches to give him all the access he wants. I swear, he could twist me into a pretzel and I'd let him as long as he keeps touching me.

He slides his fingers through my already dripping folds, swirling over my clit before he goes back to plunge his finger inside me.

I cry out, it feels so good, my head tossing back as I grind down on his finger. God, I'm so greedy when it comes to this man.

I want more, I want it all.

He pumps into me, curling around me to take my mouth with his. He kisses me over and over, his tongue tangling with mine as it plunges into my mouth. I skate my fingers through his hair, pulling him closer.

I'm half expecting him to pull me on top of him again but he doesn't. Instead, he rolls me onto my back, coming on top of me.

My shorts are off in a second, my legs automatically wrap around his hips, allowing his finger to push deeper inside me. It feels so good, stretching me, touching that spot deep inside that has me wild. He pulls out and then adds another finger as he plunges back in.

I leave one hand in his hair, yanking at the strands as the other fists into the sheets.

His cock, still in his underwear, grinds against my clit. The orgasm is already building and I make this mewling noises as my body tightens.

"Fuck, Maddie," he grits out against my lips. "You feel so fucking good."

"So…so do you," I can barely speak I'm so breathless. I'm so close that I'm starting to vibrate.

And that's when Roman eases back…

A different cry falls from my lips as I vent my frustration. It only makes Roman laugh, his low deep chuckle making my body hum.

"I don't want to take my fingers out of you so I'm going to need you to take that tank top off."

I do as he commands without thought or question, wriggling out of the fabric. His fingers brush my insides, the balled fabric of the tank clenches in my fist as I roll my hips to feel more.

He kisses a trail down my jaw, over my chest, stopping to suck a nipple into his mouth. I'm crying out again, so ready for whatever he wants to give me.

My pulse is fluttering to the rapid beat of my heart as he sucks on the other nipple and then slides lower, kissing over my belly, his tongue tasting my skin.

It's so hot, I forget to breathe. And then he slides lower. Using the flat of his tongue, he licks up my seam, my thighs starting to shake again as random words fall from my lips. Wait. Not random. I'm begging...

He licks again, swirling the tip of his tongue over my clit. That's when I lose it. Like completely lose it.

I scream, the shudder so full and deep, my entire body spasms. On and on it goes until I'm so spent, I completely relax into the bed, the tank still in my hand above my head. "Wow."

Roman pushes up on his elbows, his deep rumble bringing me back to life. "Maddie."

It's territorial, the sound of his voice. Or maybe predatorial. Either way, I reach down, finding his shoulder and trace my fingers over his neck. "Wow."

I'm capable of more words than that, but maybe not right this moment. I feel him climbing up my body, the brush of skin still making me shiver. Finally tossing the tank to the floor, I place my other hand on his back, his muscles rippling under my palm. His chest brushes my nipples and they pebble again.

"You're so beautiful," he rumbles kissing my neck. "I knew that the first moment I saw you in the light, but I never expected..."

"What?" I'm really curious. I've never done anything like this before so I've got nothing to compare Roman to, but I have this feeling. "Is this different from how it usually feels?"

"It's different," he answers. The head of his cock presses into my soaked folds, as he lets out a soft groan. "So intense."

I push him off me and onto the bed, or he lets me, as I roll with him.

If we're moving onto oral, I want to taste him too. Scooting down the bed, I kiss a trail over his six-pack abs until his cock brushes my chin. I lick my tongue over the tip, getting his pearl of precum, straight from the source. But I can taste myself too where he'd just pressed the head of his cock into me.

It's a little dirty and so erotic, excitement pulses through me again.

His hips lift off the bed as I retreat to savor the taste.

I smile, realizing that it's my turn to tease and I set about doing just that. Kissing the tip, down the shaft, along the edge of his ball sack, exploring him with small kisses and little licks.

I know he's getting impatient when his hand fists in my hair. I suck a breath between my teeth, liking the pull. The little bit of pain that comes with his desire is exciting.

I still, not moving up his shaft as he's directing. Instead, I flick my tongue over his sack.

"Fucking hell, Maddie," he groans. "That feels…"

I don't wait to see what he fills in. Instead, I wrap my lips around one of his balls and suck.

He jolts a few inches off the bed, his groan of pleasure telling me to continue even as he pulls my hair harder, wrapping the strands in his fist.

I suck on the other, taking my time before I finally heed the pulling and kiss up the long, thick length of him to sink my mouth over the tip.

He thrusts up between my lips, going so deep, the head hits the back of my throat. I gag a little, not prepared for the depth of the invasion, but I don't pull away.

I can hear him gnashing his teeth as he finally pulls back only to thrust back in. He's fucking my mouth, his body so taut, he feels like he might break.

Water starts to stream from the corners of my eyes, but I don't move. There is something so satisfying in being what he needs me to be.

My hands come to his hips and this time, when he thrusts all the way in, I tighten my grip on his skin, letting him know I'm ready for more.

A feral groan rips from his lips and then, he explodes, shooting cum down my throat. I drink it all, my nails digging into his flesh.

The second he's done, he's hauling me up his body, and crushing me to his chest. His arms wrap about me as his lips kiss the crown of my head.

I sink into him, my cheek coming to his chest as my eyes flutter closed. And that's how I fall asleep. Directly on top of him.

I wake to the early morning sun, in the exact same position where I fell asleep. On top of Roman.

I jerk awake, and his hand automatically splays out on my back, holding me close. "You all right, sweetheart?"

I close my eyes again, my fingertips dancing down his bare chest. "So good."

I feel him smile against the top of my head. "Me too."

"That's good." I snuggle deeper into him. "Because I'm kind of hoping we get to do that again." It's a bold ask for me. Not that I even really asked. More like gently suggested. But he understands as he flips us around, my back hitting the mattress before I even know what's happening.

"We're definitely doing that again. And more."

"Right now?" I feel my pulse rising, the blood rushing in my ears as I skim my hands up his back.

"Greedy girl," he rumbles close to my ear. But he doesn't sound like he's chastising me. Far from it.

I am greedy. I want every part of Roman. I run my hands over his muscular hips and down the side of his legs, his coarser hair running over my palms.

Every part of him is so masculine. I can feel myself getting wet all over again. He's already kissing a path down my body as he nips and sucks on my skin. "I love the way you taste," he rumbles into my skin.

"I like the way you taste too." My hands have run back up to his shoulders. "I don't want to wait."

He stills for a moment and then drags me a good foot down the bed. I have no idea why until he flips around, his knees settling on either side of my head as his torso stretches out on top of mine.

And then I know...we're going to taste each other at the same time.

His cock is already dangling in front of my face, and I stick my tongue out to lick it at the same moment he dives into my pussy, licking all the way down me.

My legs fall open as his cock plunges between my lips.

Its fast and messy and so perfect, our bodies tightening together, climbing higher and higher.

I break first, my cries muffled by the giant erection down my throat.

But as soon as I orgasm, he starts to cum too. When it's done, he slides to the side, pulling me with him so that we're a tangle of bodies. My eyes slide closed, I'm so ready for some more sleep.

That's when Roman's phone rings.

I lift my head, kissing his thigh. "I'm going to smash that thing with a hammer."

He laughs. "You and me both."

I roll away, covering my eyes with my arm. Roman climbs from the bed as he answers the phone. "Hello?"

I can't help it, I sigh. He leans back over, kissing my cheek. "I'll be right back, sweetheart."

I hear him walking away. At the same time, the jingle of Tom's collar alerts me I've got another visitor.

The cat jumps up on the bed, just as I'm covering my lower half with a sheet. "Morning," I say. "How was your sleep in the quiet house?"

"Meow," Tom responds, curling up by my knee.

"When should we tell Roman that you're actually Thomasina?"

The cat lets out a yawn, not at all interested in discussing the particulars of Roman.

I smile to myself as the cat's bushy tail brushes my hip. Later, is the answer. I don't want to worry about anything in this moment.

For once, I just want to relax and enjoy.
This time with Roman is more than I ever imagined possible.

CHAPTER SEVENTEEN

Roman

"It's not even six in the morning, Mason."

"And yet, you picked up on the second ring while calling someone sweetheart. Maddie, I assume."

He's got me there. He knows exactly what I've been up to. Not that it should be a surprise. I did promise to distract Maddie with seduction.

What I didn't expect was to be so distracted myself.

I meant what I said to her. What's between us is unusual. I know the word is special, but I'm trying not to even think it.

"What do you want?"

"I want to go home," he growls. "I want to fuck my wife at six in the morning while she purrs in my ear."

I let out a frustrated rumble. "I'm sorry Luke's disappearance is so fucking inconvenient for you." I never speak to Mason like this. We're a team and he is our leader. But something is breaking between us.

"That's not what I mean. I just..." Mason lets out a loud rumble. "After this tunnel, after we find Luke, let's coast."

"Coast?" This does not sound like my brother at all.

"That was always the plan. We'll have such dominance that we won't have to worry. None of the families will be able to touch us."

I frown at the phone. "We've got enough money that we can coast without the tunnel, you know. Sell the casinos. As real estate developers we don't need to interact with the other families."

He makes a noise of dissent deep in his throat. "I've spent years building the business to this moment."

"That's the Mason I know." And I'm the brother he knows. I do for people what no one else is able. Or maybe I'm just willing to do them.

"Finishing the tunnel isn't just for me." There is an ominous note in my brother's voice. "Leo's raid is complete. He brought the Vendettis in on murder charges, the blood in the car was enough, but no sign of Luke."

"What's that mean?"

"We don't know," Mason growls.

"Fuck me," I run a hand over my face. "Luke's dead, isn't he?"

Mason is silent for several seconds. "I can't say."

I close my eyes, pain making my chest ache.

"Don't give up hope," Mason's voice is softer than I ever hear it, which in and of itself is concerning.

"Fuck."

"Roman, we need to keep moving forward. Now more than ever."

My gut clenches. I know what he's asking. "You want me to take Maddie's house right now."

"Yes."

"No."

"They've brought in family from overseas. Rome, I think. I only caught one name but it's Guerriero. Warrior. The fight isn't over. We're in the death throes, and that's when things get ugly."

Death throes? Did he use those words on purpose? Is Luke really dead? My eyes squeeze shut.

He's silent, the lack of sound stretching out between us, filling with tension. Finally he breaks it. "Build her whatever you want. Spend millions."

"It's not like that. That house belonged to her grandmother. It's her last—"

"You want to help Luke? You make us impenetrable. Blocking that tunnel was the Italians last hope."

"Fuck," I spit into the phone. I know it was always the plan for me to seduce Maddie to extract what I needed, but the longer I'm with her... "If I do this..."

"You'll give all of us some piece of mind."

I hang up on my brother without answering, though I already know what I'm going to do.

I hate it, but I know my role. I've always supported my brother. He's the man who picked up the pieces of my life when no one else would or could. I trust him. Which means I'll do what he's asked. No matter what it costs me.

I walk back into the bedroom, Maddie sound asleep in my bed.

My chest fucking aches as I stare at her. I trust her too. I know Mason thinks she might be in league with the Italians. But the only person she cares about talking to is Lucia. Who is also Italian....

Shit.

I switch the phone to silent and fire off a text to Mason.

Have Lucia followed.

Lucia is the one who forced Maddie to go on that date. Maybe Lucia is responsible for all of this. My gut clenches. I will end anyone who tries to hurt Maddie...

The sheet is pulled up to just over her pubic hair, her torso on full display. She's so beautiful, she steals my breath.

I have this moment where I'm overwhelmed by this one driving thought. I don't want it to cost me her. I want her.

In my bed now, later. I want her to be happy. To trust me.

I don't say I want a future. I know I'm not the man who signs up to take care of Maddie. But another voice fills my thoughts.

I've been trained for someone like Maddie. Equipped to meet a woman's most intimate needs.

And it's not like she doesn't give back. The sex alone...

But I can't forget, this is the woman who came out to help me when I'd collapsed on the street. She would give to me what I needed, when I needed. And that makes her different. Special.

It makes me crazy to think of her putting herself in danger like that. Which is so fucking telling.

But also, she isn't like my mother. I know that. Still. How could I ever really let my guard down with anyone? The only person I've ever truly trusted is Mason.

I let out a long, frustrated growl.

Tom growls back.

I look down at the cat. "I know what you're thinking. Maddie deserves better," I whisper to the cat. He's right.

He gives a small hiss.

In her sleep, Maddie's hand rests on the cat's body, her fingers gently curling into Tom's thick fur.

Is that what's it's like to give yourself over to a woman? Tom instantly begins purring again.

I climb into the bed, pulling Maddie against my body.

She curls into me, Tom readjusting to press his length against her leg.

I bury my nose into her hair, closing my eyes and inhaling her scent.

My hand wraps around her ribs, my thumb just brushing the underside of her breast. Much as I said I didn't want to get involved in a relationship, I'd never want to hurt Maddie.

I'm so torn my chest aches.

But my brother is my brother. And Maddie is someone I've known for all of thirty-six hours.

So. Yeah. The path is clear. I just fucking hate it. I hold her tighter as I whisper. "Don't hate me for what I'm about to do."

CHAPTER EIGHTEEN

MADDIE

BY THE TIME I WAKE, Roman isn't in bed. I hear the shower in the bathroom, and rising, I start for the bathroom.

I'm not wearing a stitch of clothing, but I've stopped feeling strange about it. Nor does it occur to me that he doesn't want me in the shower with him. Is that wrong? The intimacy between us is getting intense.

I pause at the bathroom door, giving a soft knock. "Roman?"

"Want to join me, sweetheart?"

I push the door open with a smile, relieved to know I was reading this all correctly. "I do."

My body is still humming with contentment after last night and this morning. "Did you feed Tom?"

"Yes. It's about the only time he tolerates me, and honestly, the cat is always hungry. Is that normal? Is it because he was homeless?"

"Maybe," I say biting my lip as Roman turns on the secondary shower heads. I listen to them come on. There must be at least three others that fire up, hitting me from all sides. It's a luxury I have to confess I enjoy. I'd been so reluctant to leave my home, but there have been some real perks to staying at Roman's.

Warm water washes down my body a moment before Roman's hands join the rivulets of water, streaming down my skin.

I don't think I'll ever tire of his hands.

I tip my head back under the hot water, which pushes my chest out. Roman gives a satisfied growl before his mouth drops to one of my nipples.

I nip at my lip, the skin instantly puckering in his mouth. How can I be this excited after the orgasms I've just had?

But I can't seem to get enough of this man. I slide my hands down the muscles of his back, the water making his skin slick.

He cradles my body into his, his erection pressing into my belly. God, I want to know what it feels like for him to be inside me.

I've never been in love before, I've never been more than a bit infatuated with any man. I don't know if this is what love feels like, but I know that for the first time in my life, I'm in lust.

I can't get enough.

"Roman," I gasp out his name. Is it wrong to lose your virginity on the wall of a shower?

He's kissing down my belly. I know he's magic with his tongue. But I just want… "I'm ready for all of you."

He stops at my belly button, nipping the smallest bit. "I have to go out this morning, sweetheart," he says into my skin.

"Oh. Okay." But my heart contracts, and I can't help but feel a little hurt. I just offered myself to this man and he's rejecting me for errands?

He rises up, pulling me close. Our bodies press together as he whispers into my ear. "When I take your virginity, I want to make sure I can hold you after."

"Oh. Okay." The words are the same, but this time, they sound completely different. This time, they are a sigh. Because yeah, I want that too.

And perhaps my lust is a little more love than I'm letting myself acknowledge. Because the idea of him holding me after, it's just as good as the thought of having this man inside me.

He kisses me again, soft and slow and full of a promise that practically makes me sigh like a lovesick puppy.

"Want me to help you wash?" he asks.

I shake my head. "You don't have to do that. I can do it myself."

"I like taking care of you," he answers. Which shouldn't surprise me. He's crazy good at it. Where did he acquire that skill?

A little stab of jealousy pulses through me. Which is silly. Roman has likely had hundreds of willing women throw themselves at his feet. Of course, he's experienced.

He steps away, grabbing the shampoo. "That's very nice, Roman. But really…"

"Maddie," his voice has taken on a serious note that I don't quite understand. "You should take advantage of me. And just know that I will always help you."

I shake my head, trying to understand that one. He doesn't owe me anything. Yes, I helped him that first night, but he's been looking after me ever since.

And Thomasina too. Speaking of…I'm feeling guilty for not telling him the whole truth. "I really appreciate that, Roman. But honestly, once the Vendettis are in prison, I don't expect—"

He kisses me again. Harder, cutting off my words as his hands come to either side of my face. "Maddie," he murmurs against my lips. "Let me take care of you, okay?"

"Okay," I answer, even more confused. "Did something happen that you're not telling me?"

He lets out a long breath against my lips. "The call from Mason this morning…"

I still my hands, grasping his wrists. "My brother took the police to the Vendettis' place last night but there is no sign of Luke or Kate.

I gasp, clutching him even tighter. "Poor Kate. Poor Luke."

"The Vendettis were arrested last night. But they've brought in family from Italy to keep fighting…" He drops his forehead to mine. "I don't want you to leave yet." His hands slide down my neck and then cradle the back of my head. "Stay here with me where I can keep you safe. I'll take care of you too. I promise."

I melt into him. Yeah. This is definitely a bit more than lust. Maybe a lot more. "I know, Roman…"

"You do?"

"I have every confidence in you." I kiss him then, the steam of the shower adding to the heat of our embrace. "And I'll do whatever I can to help you."

"You've done enough, sweetheart."

I shake my head. I don't feel like I've done enough. In fact, I've been keeping something from him because I like having the cat here. "I have to tell you something." Thomasina is so small compared to everything he just told me, but I hate keeping the truth from him.

"What?" I feel him tense, his body turning to stone under my hand.

"The cat isn't a boy."

"What?" Air rushes from his lungs over my face.

"Tom is Thomasina. And Thomasina is going to have kittens."

"Shit." He doesn't sound angry, just surprised. "How soon?"

"Soon."

"Need more supplies?"

My mouth drops open. That's the last thing I expected him to say. "Yes. I do."

"I'll get what you need while I'm out."

I nod as he kisses me again and then sets a brisk pace of washing me and then himself.

We get out and dress, Roman leaving my side long enough to come back and press something small and rectangular into my hand. "It's a phone," he says. "Just a burner. But you can use it until we find yours."

"It's so strange," I say, wrapping my fingers around the plastic, the different shape feeling odd. "I know I had it." But still, I lift up my new phone. "Thank you."

"I've already put my number and Lucia's in there. Let's voice-program them both so you have it should you need to call one of us while I'm out."

I nod, appreciating his thoughtfulness and attention to detail. It's made this whole transition so much easier.

A half hour later, he's gone and I'm left wondering what I want to do with my day.

I miss my other animals and Thomasina seems to have gone into hiding. Picking up the phone, I call Lucia.

"Hey," she chirps. "I'm so glad you called."

"How did you know it was me?" I ask with a smile.

"Roman sent me your temporary number."

That was so thoughtful and my smile just gets bigger. "Did he really?"

"He did. Which was very nice, I have to say. Any luck finding your phone?"

"No." I shake my head, telling her about how I left the phone in Vigo's car on the night of the date, which has me launching into the whole story.

A half hour later, Lucia is still silent. I don't know that she's ever gone that long without speaking. Finally, I pause long enough that she lets out a whispered, "Holy shit, Maddie."

"I know," I sigh.

"And so Roman is what…like Vigo's competition?"

"He says that he mostly develops real estate, but they cut the Italians out of their new project and Vigo is out for revenge." Still. Now that I think on it, shooting Roman seems excessive. Or maybe not. Vincent is certifiable.

"Is Roman as wrapped up in crime as Vigo?"

"He says no."

"Just be careful," Lucia's voice tightens with worry. "I don't like any of this."

I don't tell her about the feelings I'm developing. I've got to get them straight in my own head. "On the bright side, Vigo and Vincent went to jail last night."

"Really?" Lucia sounds hopeful. "That is great news. Does this mean you're coming home?"

Roman asked me to stay and no part of me wanted to refuse.

There is a big part of me that will be sad when I go home by myself. And for the girl who'd hardly left her house in months, that's amazing.

Not only am I surviving, I'm enjoying myself. Is that only because of Roman? "Not yet," I sigh as I tell her about the Italian family members.

"It's like you stepped into the plot of a movie," Lucia adds. "But hey, if the Vendettis are in prison, and you're staying at Roman's, can Josh and I use your house?"

"Of course. What's wrong?"

"We've got some infestation in our apartment. They're spraying and we have to leave for like ten days."

Lucia's apartment is awful. She and Josh don't make much money, though, so there aren't many other options. Mrs. Higgins, my tenant, is old and I'm sure Lucia and Josh will move in once Mrs. Higgins can't live in the upstairs apartment anymore.

"You know where the key is. Help yourself."

"Thank you," Lucia gushes. "Should we take Gran's room?"

"Yes. Definitely. It's bigger and—" I hear a low groan come from under the end table on the other side of the couch.

"Crap," I mutter.

"What's wrong?" Lucia asks.

"The cat…" I get down, inching my way toward her as I catch the sound of her panting. "I think she's in labor."

"Do you need help?"

"Yes." The corner is too dark for me to see anything. At home, I have lights set up to allow me to give basic medical care to my little patients. But here… "Though I have no idea what Roman's address even is."

Lucia lets out a curse. "We're going to have to correct that. It's just weird." I can hear the concern in her voice. It has nothing to do with the cat. She thinks Roman is bad news. Then again, she liked Vigo.

I can't let her feelings sway me too much.

"I'll call you back," I tell her. "I'm going to call Roman."

"Ok," she says. "I don't leave for work for another hour and Josh is home all day. Just let us know what you need."

"I will. I love you."

"I love you too."

I hang up and instantly dial Roman, though I go straight to voicemail.

Not knowing what to do, I try again.

He doesn't pick up. But the phone almost instantly dings. I can't read the screen. "Siri, read text message."

"Text message from Roman Kincaid: 'In a meeting. Call you soon.'"

"Siri, send message. 'Thomasina is giving birth. I need your address to send to Lucia.'"

The phone dings again. "On my way."

"He's coming Thomasina," I say to the cat. "We're going to make sure you're all right."

CHAPTER NINETEEN

ROMAN

MADDIE'S CALL is a fucking relief.

I was in the middle of a meeting with the city official to start foreclosure proceedings on Maddie's property when she called. I told myself that I had to do this.

But the further into the meeting I got, the more wrong it felt. I know all the reasons I started down this road. I need to make this tunnel happen for Luke. For Mason.

My family is everything.

But I…

I'm not sure I can sacrifice Maddie's well-being for their benefit. There has to be another way.

Even knowing what the house means to Maddie, maybe she'd allow me to just buy a corner of the yard. Or lease. Or…

Something. She knows I'm trying to get Kate back too.

If there is anything left of Luke and Kate to get back.

I run a frustrated hand down my face. It's time I asked her about the house and what kind of deal she might be willing to make.

Maddie is nothing if not kind and generous.

I read her text, tell her I'm coming, and stand up from my small chair that sits in front of the inspector's desk. He stands too, his hands clasping and unclasping.

I've already handed him a generous *gift* just for sitting down with me. It's cash and it comes with no strings attached.

"When would you like me to start the proceedings—"

I hold up my hand. "Do nothing. This was just a conversation. No more."

"Of course. But you know that I'm here for whatever you need." He runs a hand over his bald head, revealing the sweat stains under the arms of his shirt. What was his name? Michaels? Has he landed himself in some kind of trouble? He shifts on his feet before he leans toward me. "Just say the word."

He's far more eager to make a deal than any other city inspector I've ever met. "I appreciate that," I give him a nod. "But you can consider my gift as exactly that. A show of appreciation for our past and future dealings."

He leans over, his brow drawing together. "I'd like to make myself as serviceable as possible."

Definitely in trouble. "I'll be in touch soon."

And then I turn and leave, quickly making my way down the parking garage of the city building.

The second I'm outside I call Maddie. "Sweetheart?"

"Are you coming?" she breathes back.

"I'm on my way."

"Thank you, Roman." The way she says it cuts through me.

And I know I'm in trouble because I respond like a moth to the flame. I'm not supposed to run around solving this woman's every problem.

Then again, maybe I've always been fighting my nature.

Am I going to hell? Committing myself to purgatory? Probably.

But either way, I cross the garage, my long strides carrying me to where Jack waits in the Honda Civic.

Climbing in, I close the door. "I need to get back to Maddie."

He doesn't hesitate, throwing the car into gear. "Everything all right?"

"The cat's in labor."

Jack hits the brakes, looks at me like I've lost my mind, and then presses the accelerator again. "The cat is a girl?"

"I'd say that's a prerequisite for being in labor." I scrub at the scruff on my cheek.

"And you're going to assist in the birthing?" I can hear the judgment in Jack's voice, the incredulity.

"Fuck you."

"Actually, I'm hoping you're the one getting fucked."

That bristles my already frayed nerves. "Mason wants me to fucking foreclose on her house so that he can get back to his wife. So don't start telling me I'm being irrational."

"What?" Jack roars, practically taking the corner out on two wheels as turns onto the street. "I was mostly joking. Of course, Maddie needs help with the birth. How could she do it alone with her sight being that poor? But your brother can't actually want you to steal the house out from under a blind woman?"

"He does." But hearing Jack say it like that calms some nerves inside of me. "I'm not doing it."

"Good. You need me to have your back? I'll tell Mason to get a fucking grip."

"He is your boss," I point out.

"Like I need this fucking job. Your father was my best friend before he went off the rails. I stay around to keep an eye on you whippersnappers. Mason thinks he knows everything and he gets too big for his fucking britches. Now are you telling him or am I?"

"I am," I answer. "But first…I have to go play midwife to a cat."

Jack laughs long and loud at that. "Yeah. Good call. You treat that girl right. She deserves it."

"Maddie or the cat?"

"Maddie. The cat is a demon. The interior of this car will never be the same."

"I think treating Maddie right involves taking in a lot of stray demons."

Jack nods. "You've got the chops for it, though kid. You're damned good at it."

"Should I be?" I never talk to anyone about this shit. But having Maddie around has brought up a lot of old feelings.

Jack shrugs. "Both your parents were seriously fucked up. I get it. You want to use what they taught you about the cruelty of the world to make yourself bigger, or to make the world better?"

I blink twice, staring over at the crusty old gangster who has been around for as long as I can remember. We've never talked like this. Never.

And I don't answer him now because it's a big fucking question. And exactly the right one, if I'm honest.

He seems to understand why I've gone silent as he zips through Vegas traffic, crossing the city in record time.

But when I get out of the car, Jack gets out too and follows me to the elevator.

"What are you doing?"

"I want to see the cat give birth. That shit's beautiful." And then he pulls a phone out of his pocket. "And, I've got Maddie's phone."

"I just gave her a burner." That I put a tracer and a recorder in. Another deception I'm not really proud to have completed.

"You can eat the cost. You're good for it."

"Where are you going to tell her it was found?"

"Vigo's car." He steps into the elevator with me.

My stomach clenches. "Maybe I should put it in the closet or something. She says she knows that she had it in the bathroom at my place."

Jack nods and hands me the phone. "Kate's phone did show a last location, by the way. She was at the Vendetti property."

"What does that mean?"

"On the run or dead," Jack replies.

I hope not. Maddie would be crushed. I pocket the phone in my jacket just before the elevator doors open and I step into the apartment.

"Thank goodness," Maddie calls. "I've been using the flashlight feature on the phone to do the best I can. She's already had two babies."

Washing my hands, I join Maddie on the floor. Looking under the table, next to the couch, I see two tiny, close-eyed, mucous-covered baby kittens.

And fuck me, Thomasina is giving birth to a third. "Holy shit."

Jack peaks out over the top of our heads. "Wow. It's like the nature channel in your living room."

I know he's rubbing salt into my wound. Crusty a-hole. But I ignore him, too involved in what's happening. Thomasina seems to be handling it very well, so I reach for Maddie's hand instead, wrapping my fingers around hers.

It's beautiful watching Thomasina. This doesn't feel like a burden at all. Which has me thinking about Jack's comments in the car.

What do I want to be? I've been so angry at my mother for the way she forced responsibility on me at such a young age, I haven't asked myself, what do I want to do with the skills that are now deeply imbedded?

Maddie's cheek comes to my shoulder. "We might be here a while. We want to make sure she's done giving birth before we leave her be with her kittens."

"Need a box or something?" Jack asks. "I can go to the pet store."

"That would be great, Jack, thank you," Maddie answers. "You've done this before."

"My sister has a cat. Not like this one. Her cat is nice."

Maddie chuckles. "He doesn't mean it, Thomasina."

My brows lift. We all know he means it. Thomasina is too busy to care though.

"Let me leave you with some lunch and then I'll make a supply run." Jack opens the fridge and starts pulling out food. Is he making us all lunch? I know that Jack had a soft spot for Charlotte, Mason's wife, but I've never seen him fix food for anyone. He clearly really likes Maddie.

I look at her profile, her lips curved into a gentle smile.

And I know the truth. Maddie would do anything for me. As if she's heard my thoughts, she turns to me. "I spoke with Lucia this morning. She has to leave her apartment for a bit. Cockroaches, I think."

"Does she need to stay here? We could put her in the unit below ours."

The smile she gives me could light all of Vegas for a night. "Maybe not downstairs. I don't think Lucia needs to hear us…" She flushes, and I rumble out a low note, wanting nothing more than to hear Maddie while I make her cum.

She clears her throat. "Since the Vendettis are in jail, I told her she could use my place."

"All right," I answer, feeling dissatisfied. I think I wanted to help Lucia for Maddie. I don't even trust Lucia. Not fully.

My attitude is a marked change, I feel the shift. I can only hope I'm not making a big mistake. Should I allow myself to fall back into these patterns after all this time?

But her hand tightens in mine. "It doesn't mean I have to stay here. I've got an extra bedroom…"

I look back at her, her mouth creased in lines of worry. My concerns disappear. Softly, I kiss her lips. "You are staying here for a while yet. We're going to tuck those Italians in a tight noose before you leave my protection."

I watch her features soften again. God, I fucking love that.

"Didn't you say you needed to move the tunnel project forward to make that happen?"

"Maybe." Why don't I just ask? *Maddie, can I put a vent on your property?* But I know the answer. As much as I bitch about not wanting to take care of a woman, I don't want Maddie taking care of me. It's my job to protect her, provide for her. Not the other way around.

"I can't sell the house. But I could probably sell or lease you some of the yard. I just need space for my animals."

My gut twists into knots. Just like that, she's offering me what I need. Just like she did that first night.

No reservation.

No one has more heart than Maddie. No one is as generous.

Just like she's letting Lucia use her place. Just like she's helping Thomasina. *You can make yourself big or make the world better.*

Maddie has chosen the latter.

"Maddie." Her name comes out like a plea, and full of the pain and indecision I feel in this moment. I was about to fucking take her house right out from under her and here she is, just giving this massive gift to me.

I hate myself.

I love her.

I feel the truth of it settle deep in my gut. She's far better than I would ever deserve. But that doesn't mean that I'm not going to try and claim her for myself.

"Maddie, moving the tunnel forward is our best chance at getting Luke and Kate back." I can only hope that Luke is still alive out there. On the run and being his scrappy self.

"Really?" The smile she gives me nearly splits her face. "That alone makes it worth it. I could use the money..."

She hesitates then and I take her hand back in mine kissing the back of it. "What do you need money for?"

She clears her throat, looking away. "Before I realized how bad my grandma was, she got way behind on her taxes. I owe the city like thirty thousand dollars in back payments. Do you think that's an amount that might be workable?"

"Maddie, we offered you ten times that."

"Yes, but for the house too. And this is just one corner of the yard, right? How big does the vent need to be?"

I shake my head. "I'll come up with a number that's fair. And while we're at it, you should be exempt from the taxes anyway. We'll get the paperwork filed."

"Really? You'd help me do that?"

Christ. This woman kills me. I'm a real estate developer. She should ask me to hang the moon for her. "I'd do a lot more than that, Maddie."

"He's midwifing a cat," Jack calls from the kitchen. "I think you ought to ask him to build you a state-of-the-art facility for your rescues. He's putty in your hands, young lady."

I glare over my shoulder at Jack.

"That's crazy," Maddie laughs.

My glare disappears. Because I'd do it. And a great deal more…

CHAPTER TWENTY

MADDIE

I COLLAPSE ONTO THE BED. How can watching a cat give birth be so exhausting? It's been hours since Thomasina birthed what I hope is the final kitten. Four babies are all tucked in with mama in the whelping box that Jack ended up going out to buy.

I stretch on the bed, my muscles sore from a day spent hunched over.

It was glorious. Nothing makes me happier than taking a creature who would have suffered alone, and giving them all the love and support they need.

My grandmother would have said that I wanted to be whatever little bird or squirrel I brought home.

Maybe she's right. Maybe I help helpless creatures because I feel like one too. I'm at the world's mercy so much of the time. But no matter the reason, I can't stop caring for the sick and wounded now. It's how I find joy.

Which is why I actually kind of love the idea of helping Roman.

Not that he's one of my wounded creatures. But still. I just want to do it for him. Show him…that he matters to me. That I care.

He walks into the room, stopping. I can feel his gaze as I stretch. "Do you ache as much as I do?"

"What are we aching for?" he asks, moving closer. My lower legs hang off the bed. His knees come between mine, softly pushing them apart. His hands settle to either side of my chest on the bed, his body leaning over mine. "Because I've had an ache that's been building for days."

My brows lift as I stretch my arms higher over my head. "Even after this morning?"

"Especially after this morning." And then he slowly lowers himself until his lips brush over mine.

He starts to pull back and I rise to keep my lips against his. All right, maybe I've been aching for him all day too.

Because he sat with me for hours watching over a cat. And when my back started to ache, he leaned against the apron of the couch, pulling my back into his chest while he rubbed my shoulders.

His scent wrapped around me then, just like it's wrapping around me right now.

He pulls away a bit further, until I can't follow any more and I collapse back on the bed with a dissatisfied click of my tongue.

He chuckles in response. But he doesn't come back to my lips. Instead, he kneels down, taking off first one of my shoes and then the other.

He slips off my socks and then slides his hands up my legs until he catches the waistband of my leggings.

I lift my ass because I have no intention of slowing any of this down. I want Roman's hands on every inch of my body and then I want to trace every angle of him.

I want to feel every ripple, every muscle until I know him as intimately as I know myself.

But he short-circuits my intentions when he gets the leggings halfway down and then plants a kiss on my lower stomach.

My fingers immediately twine into his hair, my skin pebbling with goose pimples from the kiss as a shiver races through me.

"Roman," it comes out a half sigh, half plea. I don't even know what I'm asking for.

"I'm here," he answers, pulling my leggings the rest of the way down my legs and off my feet. I'd put on cute lacy underwear this morning and I'm so glad now, as I lay underneath him in my short tank and bikini briefs.

His hands are roaming up my legs and around my thighs, his thumbs brushing along the lace. He's so close but his fingers aren't quite touching my mound, and I swear the tease makes me hotter, my panties instantly soaked.

"Mmm," he murmurs. "I love that smell."

My cheeks flush with heat and embarrassment as I try to close my legs, but he holds them open. Dropping to his knees on the floor, his shoulders only open my legs wider. And then he grabs my waist, pulling me closer to the edge of the bed, right before he dives in, licking up my still-covered pussy.

I instantly arch, all embarrassment forgotten as throbbing pleasure tightens every muscle.

He slips the panties to the side, sliding his finger against my already-swollen lips, and then he follows with his tongue.

My heels dig into his back, my body curling to give him better access.

I don't know how he manages to make me so hot so quickly, but I'm already ready to beg him for the release he can give.

But he isn't even close to letting me orgasm.

Pulling back, he flips me over onto my belly and then yanks down my underwear to my knees.

I don't argue, I don't even protest, excitement pulsing through me as he licks me again, the new angle causing a riot of sensation. "Oh God," I gasp.

His hand comes down on my ass with a playful slap. "You mean, 'oh Roman,'" he rumbles into my pussy, the hum of his voice only making me ache more.

"Roman," I gasp. "Yes. God. Please."

"Not yet, greedy girl," and then he laughs against me.

Something in the laugh kills some of the mood for me and I push my upper half up giving a cry of protest, while I rest on my elbows. "Are you making fun of me?"

He rakes his hands up my thighs. "Maddie, do you have any idea how fucking sexy you look like that?"

"Oh," I start, realizing I might be overreacting.

His hands slide over my ass, giving it a light massage before he smacks one cheek again. "And I was teasing. You're the least greedy person I know. And if the one thing you're demanding about is orgasms on my tongue, fucking sign me up."

"Ooohhh," this one comes out as a moan because he dives back in, licking from my clit all the way up until he's circling first one hole and then the other, the one I never dreamed a man would touch with his tongue. It feels amazing.

I gasp, words failing me. I never imagined being this dirty. And if I did, I had no idea I'd like it this much.

I want more of Roman. Which is likely why I'm pressing into his mouth and making little gasps and cries of encouragement as he keeps licking at my backside, the pad of his middle finger sliding over my clit.

My ass is as high in the air as my back can arch. I'm still up on my elbows, my head tipped back. I'm clawing at the sheets and I think I might be begging.

I can't even make sense of the words as he pushes a finger inside me, curling it to hit that spot that sets me off, and I cum so hard that it's a good thing he doesn't have neighbors.

I wilt into the bed, my body covered in a sheen of moisture as I try to catch my breath.

Roman is up and I hear him shucking off his clothes. "One of these days," I purr as he comes back to me, his hands trailing up my legs and over my hips, "we're going to go slow enough that I get to explore your body."

He strips off my tank top and then my bra, his lips coming to the spot where my neck meets my shoulder. "You want to touch me, baby?"

"Yeah," I answer, drawing in a deep gulp of air. "Except you turned me to jelly."

He laughs then, turning me over and picking me up to slide me further up the bed.

His climbs up my body, his knees settling on either side of my hips. Then, grabbing my hands, he places them on his chest.

His hands still cover mine as he slides them down his pecs over the ridges of his rock-hard abs.

Dipping lower, I glide my palms over his hips and down the back of his powerful thighs. I don't need his help any longer. Not that he lets my hands go.

The feel of his rippling muscles has infused me with another burst of energy. I take in the rougher feel of his skin and hair, the deep cut of the muscle about his knee, then up his powerful quads, and back over his ass, the firmness in contrast to my much softer curves. I partially sit up to continue sliding my hands up his back, my cheek coming to his upper stomach.

He threads his fingers into the long strands of my blonde hair. "Maddie."

My lashes flutter, brushing his skin. "Not nearly as erotic as what you did to me, but you feel so amazing. Your skin, you..." I kiss his belly and when I shift, his engorged cock brushes across my breasts.

My nipple puckers and I shift again, intentionally teasing the tip with my nipple.

"Fuck me," he rumbles, grabbing my other breast with his hand, holding the weight in his hand before he tweaks the other nipple.

I can feel my excitement growing again, and I wonder if he's right about me being greedy. I can't seem to get enough...

But I just came and so I kiss lower over the deep cuts in his stomach along the shaft until I get to the tip.

And then I lick, collecting up the small bit of salty goodness on my tongue.

It's his turn to be greedy and he thrusts forward, pushing the tip between my willing lips.

I slide my mouth over the swollen flesh, flicking the throbbing veins with my tongue as I use my mouth to intimately explore every inch of his cock.

I can hear him spitting and growling as I keep teasing.

Sliding my hand up the inside of one of his legs, I cup his balls in my hand, testing their weight, before I give them a small pull.

He hisses breath through his teeth. "Damn, woman, that feels good."

I smile around his cock, ready to dive back for more but he pulls away, the weight of his torso, pushing mine back down on the bed.

His hips settle between my thighs as they part to accommodate him.

I can feel the press of the head against my opening and I tense the slightest bit.

Because I'm about to lose my virginity.

CHAPTER TWENTY-ONE

Roman

Maddie tenses and I know I need to slow down.

It takes every ounce of my control, every atom of my desire to protect this woman, to ease back.

Instead, I kiss her, slowly, gentle, my brain screaming in protest.

She kisses me back, the palms of her hands sliding over my back. She relaxes at the slower pace, the soft kisses.

And even though I'm aching, dying to be inside her, there is a part of me that just enjoys.

She always tastes delicious. Apple and blossoms, crisp white wine, fresh dew. I drink her in, sliding my tongue along hers until her whole body opens to me.

Her legs relax, climbing higher on my hips.

I lower my pelvis again, nice and easy, the head of my cock sliding through her soaking-wet folds.

She doesn't tense this time, but I still ask. "You all right, sweetheart?"

"I want to be yours, Roman," she whispers back. "Make me yours."

It's all the encouragement I need as I push inside her, the head of my cock nestled in her tight heat.

My jaw clenches, the feel of her so fucking good, even as she goes rigid again. I slow my thrust, my arms shaking as I slide them under her back, pulling her tightly to my chest.

"It's all right," she whispers. "I'm good. I'm just..."

"Sweetheart," I still, brushing my lips over her forehead. "We can stop. I'd never want to hurt you."

Her arms tighten across my back. "Do it."

I hear the strength in her tone, her muscles tensing in preparation. With a quick breath, I thrust inside, seating myself inside her, even as she cries out. This isn't like her other screams.

I hear the pain in this one and I hate it.

I still again, allowing her to adjust. Fully seated inside her like this, she feels so good, I curl closer, dropping my face into the crook of her neck as I kiss her collarbone. "Just tell me when you're ready, love."

I want this to be as easy on her as possible. Maddie deserves that.

"I'm ready."

I wait another second. Two. And then I start to slide back out of her before pushing in again.

My muscles are shaking again. Not just in my arms, but over my entire body. The effort to remain slow, steady, has my body as taut as a bow string, ready to break. But I keep it light, even, because this is the sweetest torture I've ever known.

I'm meant to be here, Maddie is meant to be in my arms.

Slowly, she relaxes, her body softening as I pick up the pace. and when her hips rise up to meet mine, I know I'm being rewarded for my patience and it makes this moment even more satisfying.

"Roman," Maddie breathes out my name. "It feels so good. I… does it…"

I nip at her neck. "Just feel, baby."

Her legs tighten around me, pressing her clit just where she needs it, her walls gripping me with such force that I can't breathe, as pleasure makes me clench every muscle.

I'm spitting now, my hands gripped tight in her hair as I force myself to delay a little longer.

The effort not to cum has been herculean and my balls are so tight, I think I might explode.

Finally, Maddie lets out a scream of pleasure, her walls gripping my cock so tightly, I explode too.

Pumping my cum in her, I lift my face just enough to crash my mouth down on top of hers.

Sex, especially first time sex, should not be this good. It's crazy and amazing, and I know I'm not going to want another woman for a very long time.

Hell. I can't imagine ever.

My body is still spasming, the tremors shaking me as I collapse on top of her. I have this moment of clarity.

Maddie is mine. Maybe forever.

My eyes drift closed as my weight sinks down on her.

I try to slide to the side, worried that I'm crushing her, but she's got me in a tight embrace of arms and legs and she isn't letting me go. "Maddie."

"Just another minute," she says back.

"Can you even breathe?"

"I'm fine," she gives a breathless laugh back that does not make me confident. "I don't want this to end. It only ever gets to be my first time once."

I lift up then. Looking down at her. "Was it what you hoped it would be?" Christ, I sound like an insecure teenager.

But she only gives me a glowing smile. "It was perfect."

I know the power of good sex. And this was great sex. Amazing sex. The best.

I pull out of her, noting the blood. It's on me, it's all over her. "Fuck."

Pulling myself together, I lift her in my arms and carry her to the bathroom.

She's completely pliant in my embrace as I turn on the spray and gently wash her thighs, turning the shower head to it's softest setting as I spray warm water between her legs to relieve any soreness.

"Oh, that feels so good," she moans.

I cock a brow. "Sweetheart, you can't—"

She laughs. "I didn't mean like that. The warm water is very soothing."

I nod, but my cock still stirs. Any moan from Maddie gets the motor running.

Toweling her dry, I wrap her up as I carry her back to the bed.

She curls onto her side, and I slip in next to her. But I'm not staying. "I'll let you fall asleep and then—"

"You're leaving me?" she asks, turning back to me, worry creasing her brow.

"I'll be back, I promise. I'm going to lay on the couch for a while. Thomasina might need…" Am I being ridiculous? I don't know.

But the cat has wormed her way into my heart. Caring for her today, it's like my own form of emotional crack.

I feel responsible.

"That is so sweet. I'll come with you."

"Stay here." I kiss her back. "I'll wake you if we need you."

"Are you sure?"

"I'm sure," I murmur against her lips. "I got this. You need your sleep."

"But Roman," she's turning toward me. "This isn't your job. You don't need to sleep on the couch because I insisted on keeping the cat."

I run my hand down her back. That cat is my fault. All my fault. But I don't tell her that. "You want to know how I know the Vendettis?"

She turns back to me. "Wait? What?"

I suppose that does seem like a shift in story, but I'll circle back to what the Vendettis have to do with Thomasina. "After my mother's death, my father started a whirlwind affair with Vigo and Vincent's aunt, Maria Carcetti."

I've got Maddie's full attention, her mouth falling open. "You're serious?"

"My father did not try to operate on the right side of the law, but he wasn't a major player. In fact, he worked for the Italians." I close my eyes, drawing in a deep breath. "I don't know if he planned for this to happen, but I think he fell in love with Maria. He couldn't get enough of her. He spent nearly every penny he had lavishing gifts on her, as they very publicly carried on their affair. His boss, Toni Carcetti, was not pleased when he found out, and he killed my father and his wife."

Maddie is silent in my arms, her hands running up and down my back.

"So understand," I say, "that when I give up a few hours of sleep for Thomasina, that what you are asking of me is so small, Maddie—"

I stop when she jolts in my arms. "What's wrong?"

"It's nothing," she shakes her head. "But I would like to point out that I come with my own problems. The Vendettis..."

"Nice try, the Vendettis were always my problem. You just got caught in the middle."

"Oh."

"Now, I want you to get some sleep. I'll take care of Thomasina and her babies. Tomorrow, you should call Lucia and ask her if there is anything we're missing."

"That's a wonderful idea." Her arms are back around me, her lips finding mine.

I kiss her back, trying not to lose myself in that kiss. I could. Maddie feels so good but she's way too new at this for another round and I really should get back to Thomasina. And because, Maddie and I have all the time in the world.

I knew when I left that inspector's office that I'd made a choice. But the specifics of my choice are becoming clearer.

Maddie is meant to be mine.

And I intend to keep her for a very long time.

CHAPTER TWENTY-TWO

MADDIE

I SHOULD BE EXHAUSTED, but I can't sleep.

Something in Roman's story about his father and Maria. He said his father fell in love. That he'd gone crazy for Maria.

And then Roman compared that to himself.

Am I stretching? Trying to find meaning in his words where there is none?

Or did Roman admit that he has feelings for me?

Hope rises like a ridiculous buoy in my chest. I know it's foolish. I am not the woman that keeps Roman Kincaid.

I'm surprised I'm even the woman that gets to share his bed for a short time.

But I can't turn the hope off and so finally, I get up.

I pull on his T-shirt that's been left discarded on the foot of the bed and pad out to the living room.

Thomasina is in the whelping box, I hear her purring. "Lights," Roman commands. The lights come up and I can see Roman's arm draped down, softly stroking her head as he lays on his side on the couch. "You and Thomasina made friends."

He gives a small laugh. "We did. Finally." And then he pulls his hand out of the box and opens his arms to me. "What are you doing still awake?"

"Someone promised me cuddles after my first time," I sigh. "It's lonely in that bed."

"Come here."

I go to him without question, slipping into his arms. Our legs twine together, my arms wrapping about his bare torso, as my face snuggles into the crook of his neck.

"Better?" He brushes a kiss over the top of my head.

"Much." I can't help feeling like this is where I belong.

He pulls me even closer, his hand pressing to the spot just above my ass. It's possessive in a way that makes me feel cared for. My eyes close, so ready for sleep. "You know," he rumbles. "Thomasina's been quiet enough that I could probably bring the whelping box into the bedroom."

"Tomorrow," I murmur, not moving a muscle. Is the couch too small for two people? I know it is. I just don't care how well I sleep as long as I'm with him. "This is the most comfortable I've been all night."

I feel the laugh vibrate through his torso, his chest hair tickling my nose. I could drown in this man and I'd be happy doing it.

"Your wish is my command."

My hand slides down his side as I bury my nose even deeper into his neck. I want to ask him how he feels but it's never a question that's felt fair.

Like I'm putting some kind of pressure on him to share when maybe he isn't ready.

Or maybe I'm just afraid of how he'll answer.

So, I don't ask.

Instead, I relax into him. Well, even more than I was. But tired and comfortable as I am, the questions won't let me be. Finally, I ask one of them. "We should talk about when I go home."

"Why?" If anything, his hand presses my hips tighter to his. "There's no rush. You can stay here for as long as you need."

I shake my head against him as I debate what to say. I should leave it until the morning. But part of me has been stewing in that bedroom and I can't quite hold back the words. "Roman, you have to know that's not a good idea."

"Why not?"

I lift my head. I can hear his irritation. His voice laced with some defensiveness. "Because…"

"I know you miss your patients, but we have the kittens now and—"

I blink back my surprise. "Roman. It's not about them. It's about me. I…"

"You what?"

"I'm afraid…" I choke on the next words.

"What are you afraid of, love? Whatever it is, you know I can fix it."

He is not making this conversation easy. I press deeper into his arms, my hands clinging to his skin. How can he save me from the heartbreak he himself will bring? I feel it as surely as I feel the skin of his back. Roman Kincaid will break me. But I don't know how to say any of this. "I'm not good at having lovers."

I feel him relax, his muscles loosening. "Not true. What happened tonight was next level."

That makes me flush with heat. It's amazing to know. And it calms some of my reservations. "Let me rephrase. I've never had a casual sex thing. I've never had any sex at all. I don't know how. I…" I'm stumbling again, trying to make him understand that my emotions are already involved.

"Fuck. Maddie." But maybe I said enough. Because his hand finds my chin and then he's tipping my face up a moment before he captures my lips with his. It's sweet and sexy all at the same time, especially when he opens my mouth, sweeping his tongue against mine.

My body heats, the kiss growing desperate as I cling to him.

It goes on and on, sleep completely forgotten, until Roman finally pulls back. I cry out a small protest.

"Baby, you're too new at this, we have to stop now."

"I don't want—"

"We can't get too deep tonight, your body needs to recover and you need your sleep." Then he gives me another soft kiss, meant to soothe, not excite. My mouth clings to his. "But this isn't casual for me, either."

I shake my head. It can't be true. "Nobody stays around to love me, Roman." I didn't mean it like that. Not like he has to be in love. "Not that I expect you to love me like that. I mean caring—"

He hugs me tight to his chest. "I know what you meant and it's not true. Lucia loves you. Your grandmother did too."

"I love them both too."

"So maybe everyone doesn't choose to be in your life. Maybe it's just a few. But the people who choose it, Maddie, I think they choose it all the way. No reservations. No hesitation."

He's not talking about himself, is he? Again, I don't ask. I've already put enough pressure on him. "You can't know that."

"I do know that. Just like I know that you love with your whole heart. Without reserve, you give to every person you love. You inspire loyalty, Maddie, and you give it too."

My shaking fingers touch his cheek. No one has ever said such beautiful things to me. "Roman…"

"You need your sleep, sweetheart. Let's finish discussing this in the morning."

I grimace. Sleep is the last thing I need now. Because as much as he's said, I find myself wanting to say more. So much more. The words I've been holding back fall from my lips. "I think I might be in love with you."

Shit. I didn't mean to say that either.

He kisses me again, a chaste kiss that leaves me feeling empty. It's not even close to enough. "Maddie. You stay here as long as you want. And count me among the people who will give you the shirts off their backs. Understood?"

I nod, laying my head back down, fighting ridiculous tears. This is why I should have waited. Or kept quiet. I'm too tired, too raw, to keep my chin up. On the surface, it all sounds great. But there is so much he didn't say.

He didn't tell me he loved me back.

I knew he wouldn't, but still, I'd hoped…and I'd promised myself I wouldn't pressure him to give more than he wished.

With a sigh, I turn, facing out so that our bodies are spooned together.

Thomasina gives a small meow and I reach down into the box, giving her a small pet, before I tuck my hands under my face.

I went and fell in love.

And the man I picked just told me about how much loyalty I inspire.

It's great and all, but…

I should have stayed silent. Should have stayed in the bed.

Losing your virginity can override even the most sensible person and even my gran says I was lacking in that department.

"Maddie," Roman rumbles behind me. "What's wrong?"

I won't make the same mistake again. We're done talking, especially about my feelings. If we keep going I'll likely cry, and I don't know a ton about relationships, but I do know that will not help my cause. "Nothing. Good talk."

His hand slips from my arm to my belly, and then lower, dipping between my legs. I'm only wearing his T-shirt, which means his fingers slide along my bare pussy.

Even now, hurt feelings, aching body, I shudder in response, my body instantly responding.

His lips come to my ear. "Don't pull away, sweetheart. Don't give up on me."

My pulse explodes in my veins, blood rushing in my ears.

I'd give him every piece of myself if he'd let me.

His hand stills, just cupping my pussy as he continues to nuzzle that spot on my neck. "I'm not giving up on you," I say. "I never give up on anyone."

"I'd figured that one out all on my own."

I smile turning my head so that his nose is against my jaw. "But I also know that I'm too much for so many and I don't want to overwhelm you."

"I'm a man, Maddie. I can take anything you give, any burden you need."

I shake my head. It isn't true. "I'm trying to know when enough is enough, when I need to give you space, not more of myself."

His other arm is under me, wrapping tighter about my torso. "I don't want space. I want you."

That quiets some of my fears and I close my eyes, sighing into him.

Did he tell me that he loved me? No.

But those words. For tonight…they are enough.

CHAPTER TWENTY-THREE

MADDIE

AND BY THE NEXT MORNING, I turn into a chicken.

Even though he said we'd talk more today, I don't ask Roman anything else as we have breakfast. I take a shower, and for the first time since I came here, he doesn't join me.

This shouldn't be a big deal. People shower alone all the time. It's not usually a group event. Then again, most people don't have showers with six shower heads.

I've learned the layout well enough that I don't need his help, but I can't shake the feeling that I messed something up last night.

Why did I have to go confessing that I was falling in love?

I get out of the shower, dry off, and after wrapping the towel around my body, I sit down to brush my hair.

I wish I could blow it out. I mean, I can blow-dry my hair. But I need someone else to really style it.

I could try...

The lighting in here is amazing, even better than the rest of the house and when I lean close...

I start to work at the strands using a large round brush to straighten with just a big curl at the end, then Roman enters. I turn off the blow dryer with a sigh, sure I'm not doing a great job.

"What are you up to?"

Considering how much I've already confessed, I think it's best I don't say, *trying to look pretty for you*. So instead, I go for snark, which is not my thing at all. "Umm. I'd say it's obvious, isn't it?"

He stops behind me. "Is it? I've never seen you dry your hair before."

I let out a sigh. God, I suck at this *hiding my feelings* thing. "I bet the other women you've dated dry their hair."

His hands come to my shoulders, sliding along my skin. "I don't really date. So, I wouldn't know."

My brows scrunch at his words. "You have satchels of overnight products prepped in your bathroom."

"Those aren't for dates," he answers, gently taking the blow dryer from my hand. "To be clear, they are for women I convince to come back here for a single shared night. And since we're being honest," he takes the brush from the other, "what you and I are doing is in keeping with that, because I didn't ask you out on a date either.

And then he starts to dry my hair. I blink my eyes several times because, those words hurt. We didn't go out on a date. He did just convince me to come back here with him. I'm a hook-up…

The sting reverberates through me a moment before my mind rebels. He told me not to give up on him. I reach out for the counter to steady myself as I try to get my emotions and thoughts back in check.

I can feel him rolling the brush through my hair, as he holds the strands against the dryer. He works around my head, the steady hum of the blow dryer creating a pause in our conversation as I try and pull myself back together.

I can see him creating a sleek coif. I tilt my head, leaning closer. It's perfect.

But somehow, I no longer want to look like every other woman.

He doesn't notice or doesn't acknowledge my change of mood as he finishes the task, switching the dryer off.

I look down at my lap. He reaches my chin, tilting my face back up. "But Maddie," he says like no time has passed.

"Yeah?"

"You are completely different in that none of them have ever been invited to stay longer than a night."

"Oh," I blink back my surprise, turning to face him. Because he gave me an indefinite invitation that was completely at my discretion.

"And you're different from them in that you don't need makeup or hair styles to make you beautiful. You are stunning just as you are, sweetheart."

"Oh." I stand then, my body pressing into his. He steps back long enough to tug his T-shirt off and then jerks the towel off my body, before he pulls me close. "In that case," I say, trying to catch my breath as our skin slides together and I wrap my arms around his neck. "Do you want to mess my hair back up?"

He barks out a laugh as he uses his free hand to shuck down his athletic pants. "I'm going to mess it up so good, baby."

That makes me laugh for a second before his lips crash down on mine.

His tongue is in my mouth, his hand wrapping under my ass as he lifts me in his arms.

My legs come around him, the tip of his cock already pressing into my folds.

The moment he pushes into my entrance though, I wince a bit. It's not like yesterday, it doesn't burn. But the skin is tender.

Roman eases back, seeming to understand. Taking two steps forward, he sets me down on the bathroom counter.

He kisses me again, his tongue teasing mine before his mouth slides lower, down my jaw, along the pulse of my neck, over my collarbone and down to my chest.

He sucks one nipple into his mouth, palming the other. Gasping, I arch into his touch.

But he doesn't stop, he keeps kissing lower over my belly, along the seam of my leg, and across my mound, only stopping when he reaches my clit.

I'm wide open now and dripping as he swirls his tongue over the sensitive bud. He's so good at this, I've completely forgotten about the pain. Soreness be damned. I want Roman inside me.

But his tongue is working my clit and I'm having a difficult time telling him to stop. The man is magic with his tongue.

My fingers are gripping his hair, pulling as I cry out. He slides a finger inside me, and then another. I'm sure he's testing my soreness but I'm way too far into this to care about a little pain.

I start pulling his hair harder, tugging him back up my body.

He obliges, filling both of his hands with my ass as he pulls me to the edge of the counter.

My legs wrap around him as his cock slowly pushes back inside me. He eases in, likely giving me a moment to adjust. Much as I appreciate it, we both groan out our pleasure when he's finally buried deep inside me.

I can feel him pushing against that magic spot that has me arching to take even more.

Hands on my hips, he eases out and then thrusts hard back in. Pleasure rocks through me as he sets a pace that makes my head spin and my body vibrate. I'm barely balanced on the edge of the sink, one of my hands wrapped around a faucet while the other digs into his shoulder, my nails gouging into his back.

But the faster we go, the harder it is, the better it feels.

My moans grow louder, sharper, until I'm begging him, talking more and more as I get closer to my orgasm. "Harder. Yes. Like that. Oh Roman. Please. Fuck me."

I didn't even know this side of me existed.

But Roman only goes faster, pounding me with a force that I can't get enough of. "You want it harder, baby?"

"Yes. Yes." My nails only dig deeper and then with a flurry of thrusts that have my head snapping back, I explode around him, scratching down his skin.

He's right behind me, cumming with a roar as he continues to pump into me like a piston.

I'm still holding onto him, feeling the jerking pulses of his body as he finally slows the pace. "That was…"

His forehead comes to mine, his arms wrapping around my back. I let go of the faucet and tip my weight forward, against him, only to realize that every muscle in my body might be sore.

Totally worth it.

"Fantastic," he rumbles as he lifts me off the counter and carries me into the shower.

"I just got out of the shower, you know."

"Did someone get you all dirty again?"

I laugh, and then run my hand over his neck. "You could have come with me the first time." My hurt is showing but I can't hold it back.

I know he hears it as he squeezes me tighter. "Sorry I didn't join you, sweetheart. Mason called…"

"Any news?"

"About Luke and Kate? No. But he does have some lease terms he wants to run by you."

"Lease terms." It sounds so unimportant after what we just did.

Roman rinses me off, spraying cool water between my legs this time to reduce any swelling, before he soaps himself up.

We both get out to dress, conversation soft and easy, all my worry gone for the moment.

Roman puts my clothes on first, an easy A-line dress, and then pulls on a pair of athletic pants slung low over his hips. "I've got a bit of research to do," he says as he opens the door and steps out into the hall. "But I'll be here all day— What the fuck?"

I immediately tense, freezing in the middle of the room.

"I told you I wanted this wrapped up."

"You don't get to just show up at my place, Mason. Christ. How long have you been here?"

"Long enough," Mason mutters and my face heats. Did he just hear…

I've learned that I'm rather loud during sex. Not something I knew about myself, but there you have it. If Mason was here, he heard everything.

I spin toward the bathroom, intent upon hiding.

But Roman grabs my hand, stopping me before I flee. "Maddie, Mason wishes to speak to you far more than he does me."

I shake my head. My face surely bright red. "Roman."

"It's all right," he answers, pulling me toward the doorway. "He's here to write you a big check."

Somehow that doesn't make me feel any better.

Because even with my vision as it is, I can see enough to make out the large red scratches decorating Roman's back because he isn't wearing a shirt.

CHAPTER TWENTY-FOUR

Roman

Maddie's cheeks are shades of red I've never seen before, the blush spreading down her chest.

Is she embarrassed?

She shouldn't be. What we just did was fucking beautiful. Never in my life have I had sex like that.

I've made plenty of women cum. I'm a giver in bed.

I've made them scream, but with Maddie, every feeling, every touch is amplified.

Mason is glaring at me like he knows. I didn't agree to this lease deal with my head. It was a decision of the heart.

Business would demand that we proceed with the foreclosure. We could get the property dirt cheap and not have to worry about an owner of the property backing out of the lease or being a nuisance.

But I can't do it. I won't be the person who hurts Maddie.

I turn toward Maddie because she's trying to tug her hand out of mine. But that only makes Mason rumble.

Glancing over my shoulder, I note that his gaze is fixed on my back.

Glancing down I see the scratches Maddie has slashed across my skin. Mason doesn't assume the decisions are being made with my heart but with my cock, by the way he's glaring at the marks.

It's not wrong.

But it's more than just the sex, and I know it. It's the way I'm protective of her. The way I run to her every time she calls.

It's the amount of time I spend on my knees because the sound of her cumming is the best sound in the entire world.

I turn back to Mason, standing in front of Maddie. My glare should say it all. *Play nice.*

I love my brother. I'd die for him. Kill for him. But hurting Maddie is a bridge I won't cross. And he's going to have to respect it. This is new territory for us. Mason is my idol. My father figure. But I'm a man and this is my woman.

I suddenly understand my brother Leo a great deal better. He's been fighting Mason to gain some basic rules of respect for a long time.

But I'm not sure Mason is getting the memo.

He rises, his face black. "As I told Roman, this is a ridiculous amount of money for the size parcel we are discussing."

"Oh," Maddie whispers behind me. "I didn't realize. I'm sorry." Her hand comes to my back, her palm flattening out as her fingertips dig into my skin.

My arms cross over my chest. Mason is not an easy man. And all of his softness is reserved for his wife.

But he's going to have to include Maddie on his very short list of people he treats with care. Or we're going to have real problems.

"Don't be sorry, sweetheart. The deal should be beneficial to both parties. That's how deals work," I stare at Mason, daring him to argue.

"It's our job to pay her back taxes now?"

"Oh," Maddie catches her breath. "Roman told you."

Mason lifts a brow. He knows that I learned about the back taxes long before Maddie told me.

I bare my teeth, telling him without words to shut the fuck up. I'm going to have to come clean with Maddie. I know it.

But I don't need Mason starting a trail of bread crumbs that I can't control. My hands drop to my sides, my fists clenching. "I'm going to get a shirt."

"Good idea," Mason fires back, all spit and vitriol in his tone. "Pretend like you have a job and it's a Tuesday at eleven in the morning. Oh wait. You don't need to pretend. You do have a job and it is Tuesday at eleven."

"Fucker," I say back. Maddie's hand is still on my back, her breath warm on my skin. I reach behind me and grab her hand, pulling her into the bedroom with me.

"Miss Reid can stay," Mason says as we leave.

I feel Maddie's hand shake in mine. Fuck that.

Mason is a shark in business. I don't blame her for being concerned. I pull Maddie into the bedroom, knowing there is no way I'm leaving her alone with Mason. Letting go of her hand, I close the door, and cross to the dresser to grab a T-shirt, socks, and sneakers. "I need to have a word with my brother."

I barely contain my anger as I say the words.

"Of course," she answers, her arms wrapped around herself. "Should I go in the bathroom so you have some privacy?"

My shoulders drop. Maddie is one of the most honest and considerate people I know. "No, love. I'll walk Mason out."

"And the papers?"

"He can leave them here," I call loud enough for my brother to hear. "We'll worry about signing them later."

"This is just the first step, like a purchase and sale," Mason answers through the closed door.

"Then perhaps you should have been more polite," I grit back.

I hear Mason sigh. Maddie's hand comes to my arm. "Thank you, Roman. But I can sign today. It's no problem."

And she starts around me, heading toward the door.

"I will be right out," I tell her, shrugging on the shirt. There is no way I'm leaving Mason alone with her for more than a few seconds.

My secrets aside, my brother is not bullying her into anything.

But when I come out, he's got her hand in his, leading her toward the counter. "My apologies, Maddie." His tone now soft and gentle. "I miss my wife and I'm afraid it's made me...difficult."

"You're always difficult," I gripe back, sitting on the couch to put on my socks and shoes.

"True," Mason smiles, helping Maddie into a chair. "Let me read the clauses out loud to you so you know what you're signing."

"Thank you very much," Maddie answers. "I don't know what Roman has shared but I can see the outlines of things. Blurs. But reading is not something I'm able to do under the best of circumstances."

Mason sets himself to explaining each clause, Maddie nodding along. When he's done, he hands her a pen. She wraps her fingers around it. "Could you...would you mind just placing my hand in the appropriate place?"

I'm next to her, my hand clasping her free one. Maddie has gotten better and better at maneuvering my apartment. It's times like this, I'm reminded of how much more difficult life must be for her.

I bend over, brushing my lips over the shell of her ear, even as Mason places her right hand just above the line for her to sign.

His eyes meet mine over the top of her head. Is he starting to understand how vulnerable Maddie is? And, even though she has every reason not to be, how generous she is too? She came back out for Mason's comfort.

Or did he just want her to sign? It's tough to tell with my brother.

She signs the paper and then gently sets down the pen. "Roman has mentioned Charlotte several times. Please send her my regards. And I sincerely hope you make it back to her very soon."

"Thank you, Maddie."

She hesitates for a moment, her fingers squeezing mine. "And thank you for your efforts to find Kate."

"I think we might be thanking Kate, if she patched Luke back up." Mason runs a rough hand through his hair with a quick glance at me. Does he know something I don't? Has he heard from Luke? His voice wasn't filled with the worry I'd heard last time Mason and I spoke about our cousin.

Maddie nods. "I'm sure she did. But my guess is that, just like me and Roman, Luke is taking care of her now." She squeezes my hand like she's thanking me.

The words hit me like a gut punch.

"Maddie, I'm going to see Mason out."

She nods. "Of course."

I bring her hand to my lips, brushing her knuckles with my lips, before I let her hand go.

I walk to the elevator, Mason following. I don't say or do a thing until the doors close. Without warning, I take a swing, clocking him in the fucking jaw.

His head snaps back as he falls against the wall.

Leo and Mason go rounds regularly, but I rarely physically fight with either of my brothers. They're so much older than me, it's not been our dynamic. Luke and I were a different story. We fought like two junkyard dogs.

But today, the rules change.

I let Mason recover, squaring my shoulders as he shakes off the hit and charges toward me.

He's going to ruin his Armani suit, but he doesn't seem to care, as he grips me around the waist, crashing my back into the elevator wall, his shoulder pushing into my solar plexus.

I get another good hit in his face, hard enough that he stumbles back, and then it's me who grabs him around the chest and sends him back into the far wall.

We're going to have to replace the elevator.

"What the fuck, Roman?!" Mason roars as he gets me a good one right in the eye.

I let go of his body, but my face is up in his face. "You are going to play nice with Maddie from now on, is that understood?"

"It's a billion-fucking-dollar deal."

A calm I haven't felt my entire life washes over me. I don't care.

I don't care about the money. The casinos can fuck off. I love my family, but Maddie is my future.

I've been groomed to be Mason's replacement. I'm good at it. Good at the details. At making deals, at running companies.

But that isn't what I want. It's on the tip of my tongue to just quit. Leave the whole thing.

But the doors slide open, Jack leaning against the Civic.

He takes one look at us and chuckles. "I see you had that talk."

"Yeah," I answer. "We had that talk. The one where Mason is going to mind his manners and treat Maddie like she's his next sister-in-law and not some throw-away pawn in his Las Vegas power game."

"Our Las Vegas game," Mason points a finger at me.

"Is that the game where I try to fuck over the sweetest, most innocent woman on the planet? The very one who risked her life for me? Who signed those papers for you? You can fucking have that game, Mason. I don't want it."

And then I turn and get back into the elevator, punching the button. "And I want an update about Luke. I know you know something. I could hear it in your tone."

I catch Mason's shocked stare right before the doors slide closed. I let them close.

I'm going back upstairs to hold the woman I love. I think it's time I told her how I feel.

CHAPTER TWENTY-FIVE

Maddie

Thomasina is in her box as I lay on the couch, feeding her bits of plain chicken. A mother needs her strength, and this part, I can do.

She eats every bite I give her, even as she lays on her side nursing the kittens. I stroke her head, softly encouraging her. "Tomorrow, we'll get some more fish for you, sweet girl. You need lots of good protein."

Thomasina keeps purring. The elevator doors open and I hear Roman's footsteps across the floor. He doesn't say a word as he comes toward me.

I pull my hand from the box, propping up on one elbow. "Everything all right?" I ask, cocking my head as I listen to his sure steps. His energy is off…

"Fine, my love," he answers. "Very good."

He sits down on the couch, pulling me into the hollow of his body, so that I'm wrapped up in hold.

His hand comes to my hair, stroking down the length, even as he drops a kiss on the tip of my nose.

He's called me sweetheart a million times. And he's even called me love. But never *my love.*

I pause over the choice of words, my heart rising in my throat. "You're sure?"

"I'm great." His nose rubs over the tip of mine. I reach up to cup his face, wanting his lips on mine.

But when I touch the side of his face, he winces the slightest bit. I can feel the swelling. "Roman!"

"It's nothing." He takes my hand from his face, bringing my palm to his lips.

"It's not nothing. You need ice. What happened?"

"Mason and I had a little talk."

I'm pushing off the couch so that I can get up and get ice, when I stop… "Talk? Which part of your face did you use for this conversation?"

He gives a low chuckle, bending down to kiss my lips. "The wrong one, clearly."

"But…" I didn't have siblings and certainly not brothers. "Is this normal?"

He sighs. "For grown men to solve their differences with their fists? In my family, I'm afraid so. Mason, Leo, and I were without parents at a fairly young age. We might be more wild than most."

"Oh." But some kind of heat pools low in my belly. I like wild…

Roman's brand anyway. It's the perfect combination of safe and free, and I've never felt more able to let my own inhibitions go.

He hears the change and his light kisses deepen. Much as I'd like to lose myself in that kiss, I push at his chest. "Ice."

He lets me up and I cross to the fridge, fumbling a bit with the ice drawer. "Need help?"

"I'm helping you," I say, my exasperation evident. I finally get enough ice in the towel, and I cross back to him. I don't give him the towel though, instead I lift it to his face. "What was this fight about?"

I've got some idea. Mason was not pleased with the deal Roman offered me. It was obvious.

"It was about how Mason thinks he is the boss of everything."

My brows lift. That doesn't really help. "Like you?"

"He is my boss. But not yours. And when he speaks to you, he won't do so like he's talking to an errant employee."

"Roman," I gasp. "You did not need to fight with your brother on my account."

"Yes, I did." And then he pulls me close.

"Really. I'm fine. I—"

"No one is going to speak to you like that. You will get the respect you deserve."

I melt into him. I don't need people to respect me. I'd prefer they didn't show disrespect.

But Roman doesn't seem to be finished. "Look, Maddie, there's more I should tell you."

I pull my chin back, trying to understand. "About Mason?"

"Mason. Me. Our future."

He tightens his hands in my dress. I don't mean to, but the ice pouch drops a bit. "Our future?" There is that hope again.

But he lets out a long tired breath, the kind that makes me wince. I don't think I'm going to like what he's about to say.

"Before we talk about all of that, can I just tell you how I feel—"

But he's interrupted by Thomasina's meow. It sounds off. Like she's hurt or scared. I'm spinning, bending down. I see the blur of her jumping from the whelping box.

I reach a hand down to her, realizing she's got one of the kittens in her mouth. Running one hand down her back, I grab for the kitten in her mouth. But when my fingers wrap about the little body, I gasp. The kitten's body isn't warm enough.

Thomasina, lets the baby go, meowing again. She's asking for my help.

"What is it?"

I don't answer as I place my finger by the little one's mouth. "Not breathing."

"Shit."

He drops down on his haunches his hands coming to my back.

But I'm already working, stroking the kitten's body, gently squeezing to stimulate its little heart.

With a sputter, I feel the moment the kitten draws breath.

Thomasina meows again, but I keep working, making certain that the baby doesn't stop.

"What should we do?"

"Can we take the kitten to Lucia?"

Roman let's out a frustrated breath. "The vet clinic is closer. Maybe we should go there?"

"Good idea," I breathe, rising as I continue to rub the kitten, keeping its heart and lungs working.

Thomasina follows me and Roman as he gets the carrier that Jack brought the very first day. It's in the closet.

He carries it back toward the whelping box. "You keep massaging the kitten. I'll get Thomasina in…somehow."

"Just put the kittens in the back and she'll follow." I keep the sick kitten in my hand as Roman loads up the other cats.

Picking up his phone, he places the call and then we're off in the elevator.

I realize this is the first time I've left his apartment since I've arrived. I'm used to remaining in one place.

But as we go down the elevator and into the parking garage, I'm aware that the change of scenery from my house has been nice and going out will be even nicer.

Lucia was right. My world has gotten so small after the death of my grandmother. It's nice to let it grow, to have new places and people. More than nice.

Roman opens my door, helping me into his car. Thomasina and the rest of the kittens go in the back.

He gets in last and starts the car. "They'll see us right away," he tells me as puts the car in reverse.

"Thank you, Roman," I don't even know how to tell him how much I appreciate this.

"How's the kitten?"

"Still breathing." I keep massaging, the little body still warm and moving in my palm.

"Good," he rubs his hand down my arm as he drives through the bright sunshine.

This is way more than any man would want to take on. The fact that he's doing it for the blind woman who professed her love the night before is shocking.

But I don't say any of this because I'm focused on the kitten.

Any maybe still a little afraid to start a repeat of last night. I can't take the rejection again when Roman doesn't share my feelings.

We arrive at the clinic and Roman is out of the car, grabbing Thomasina and then helping me out.

I have that moment where I hate that he has to help me. That I'm a burden to him. But his arm comes around me, the carrier in the other hand.

He seamlessly helps me inside and we're whisked into an exam room. It's small, and Roman sets the carrier down on the bench seat.

"Everything still good?"

I nod even as I bite my lip. "I'm worried we'll lose this little one. They don't all make it. It's a hazard of the business."

"You take on the hurt of their loss so that they can hurt less," Roman whispers against my temple as his arm wraps around me. "It's one more way you're so generous, Maddie."

I smile even as the door opens for the vet tech to come in. "Welcome back to LV Animal Care. I'm Mike."

"Hi Mike," I say, turning toward him, my brows pulling together at both his choice of words and his tone. There is a hostility I don't understand even if the words are pretty standard. And what does he mean by welcome back? "Nice to meet you."

He clears his throat. "What's wrong with this one?"

It's in the way he says one…like it's one of many.

"The kitten stopped breathing. It…"

He lets out a heavy sigh. "You know there are professional vets and techs for a reason."

I look at him, not understanding.

"I know you're the woman who dropped off the hodgepodge of animals at our clinic." I tense, hearing his disapproval. Not many people see value in what I do. Or in me. I'm used to it, but also, it's easier to avoid it most of the time. I've never been much of a fighter and I don't want to try. "Not one of them had a care plan. They were a nightmare for the vet school."

"Actually, that was me," Roman answers, his voice menacingly deep. "And all the animals were being regularly treated by a licensed vet."

"Really? A vet would have sent notes. Files. Your operation looks like nothing but a mom-and-pop shop."

I open my mouth to argue, but close it again. It's only a "mom" animal hospital. There is no "pop."

I can see his outline, thanks to the exam lighting, but I don't see the tray that's on the counter. My hip catches it, and it goes crashing to the floor.

"Oh! I'm so sorry," I say, bending down. With the kitten still in one hand, I start feeling on the floor for the tools I've knocked down.

I hear Roman's rumble next to me, his disapproval, and I wince. I know I'm a lot and the reason I stay at home so much is because it's so much more obvious when I'm out how much I struggle.

If Roman didn't want to ditch me before, he certainly does now.

But he doesn't say a word to me. Instead, he talks to the tech. "They shouldn't have been hanging over the edge like that. They're a hazard to anyone."

Mike lets out a disagreeable grunt. "And people like her shouldn't be caring for animals."

I wince as I hold the small kitten to my chest.

But before I can even say a word, Roman's arm is around me. "What did you just say to her?"

"Look. I'm just calling it the way I *see* it." Mike's tone drips of self-importance, while I try to shrink into my dress. "Some of those animals were in real distress and here we are again."

"None of them were in distress." I argue. Thanks to Lucia's help, all my patients had excellent care.

But Roman has the exact opposite reaction. "Is that how you see it?" he grits out.

"Yeah. It is."

"Want to know how I see it?" The tension rolls off Roman in waves. "I see a little man with an even smaller mind."

"You can't talk to me like that," Mike says back, his tone taking on a whining quality that grates.

"You thought she was someone you could belittle to make yourself feel better."

"I…I did not…"

"But you are going to answer to me. I happened to notice your accusations were rather vague. Which animals were in distress? Tell us, Mike."

Mike takes a giant step back. "I…"

Roman moves forward right in Mike's face. Even I can tell that Roman is much taller. Larger in every dimension. "That's what I thought. You know, she's twice the caretaker you'll ever be. Apologize."

My mouth is hanging open as I listen to this exchange. Roman is not acting like a man who is going to bolt. He sounds like he's defending me. My heart swells.

"Sorry."

The door opens, the vet stepping inside. "Mr. Kincaid, is everything all right?"

CHAPTER TWENTY-SIX

MADDIE

ROMAN GLARES at Mike and then turns to the vet. "Your tech accused Maddie of negligence in her care of the birds and squirrels that came here."

"What?" the vet breathes. "Mike?"

"There were no care plans." He sounds like a sulky teenager, but my face is still hot and I'm sure I'm various shades of red. He's not the first veterinary professional to tell me I've no business caring for animals.

Part of me has always believed them.

But then I'd find some wounded creature and I'd think to myself… if not me, then who… If I walk away, that might mean this little creature dies.

And so I'd take the bird with a broken wing or the squirrel with the broken leg home. My grandmother would sigh about my heart being bigger than my smarts.

The vet lets out a frustrated sigh. "It's not true. I got the plans verbally from Dr. Anderson myself. She took the time to go through each case with me."

"Lucia." I should have known. I'm not sure what I did to deserve such an amazing friend but my shoulders wilt in relief.

"But—" Mike starts.

"You're dismissed."

Mike huffs out a breath, but leaves the room, the door closing with a thud behind him.

Roman's hand is at my back again, his body close enough that I can feel his heat.

"My apologies," the vet clears her throat. "I'm Dr. Stevens."

With a nod, I hold the kitten closer, still feeling awkward and nervous. "It's nice to meet you."

Roman's other hand comes to the underside of mine, like he's holding the kitten too. "Should we let Dr. Stevens examine the patient?"

With a wincing nod, I hand the baby over, waiting while Dr. Stevens completes her checkup. "Tell me what happened that's brought you in."

"The kitten stopped breathing," I say. "I used massage to stimulate the heart and lungs again."

"Good thinking," Dr. Stevens says, "Not everyone is able to do that."

I really appreciate her kind words. Roman gives me another gentle squeeze. I take in several slow breaths as I wait, trying to clear out my worries.

"There's not much to be done," Dr. Stevens hands me the kitten back. "Heart rate is normal, number of breaths per minute are not elevated. Weight is fine, but I'd keep a careful eye on that."

"I will." Roman has a kitchen scale. It will only take a minute. I'm sure Roman will help me.

"Overall, I'm afraid, this is a wait-and-see kind of situation."

I nod, snuggling the kitten back against my body. I'm not surprised to hear her say that. "Thank you."

"I hope you weren't hoping for more from me."

I shake my head. "This is not my first patient that's given birth. I know how tenuous these first days are. I just wanted to make certain there wasn't an obvious health issue with this little one. It's always a worry that there is something wrong with the heart or lungs."

"I agree. It was smart to bring the kitten in. And you're welcome. Though, I'm pretty sure, I should be thanking you."

"Why is that?"

"Your animals have provided endless educational opportunities for us. Dr. Anderson's plans were excellent, and a different methodology from our own. In addition, we rarely get to have animals in the various states of healing for our students to look at comparatively."

"Dr. Stevens," I start, worried she's just being nice. "You don't have to—"

"I do. Have to. And just so we're clear, we have several open positions in the vet school for associate professors. If you ever find yourself in need of a job, call me."

I blink back my surprise, my heart swelling in my chest. It's more than I'd ever hoped for. Not having finished college, I'm not even sure I'm qualified but the offer still takes my breath. To think of someone wanting me... "Thank you."

Roman and I walk out of the exam room, the kitten now rooting around on my chest. Poor thing is likely hungry.

I brush my hands down it's little back. "I'll hurry. As soon as we're in the car, I'll give you back to Mama."

Roman's got an arm around me, his other hand holding the carrier as he guides me through the waiting room and down a short hall.

We're almost to the door when someone else stops us. "Roman."

"Alex," Roman rumbles. Then he squeezes my arm. "Maddie, this is Alex. He's the one who picked up your animals."

I stop, all my insecurities coming back. My first conversation with Alex wasn't the easiest one. He was barking on the phone to Roman, Lucia was snarking at Alex.... "Hi," I softly reply, my chin dipping to my chest. "It's nice to meet you."

"And you. I'd shake your hand, but I see they're full."

I smile at that, thinking that Alex is actually much nicer than Mike.

"Thank you again for all your help. I don't know what I would have done if you hadn't collected my rescues. And my apologies about Lucia. She is the most wonderful person but she's not afraid to express herself."

"No need to apologize. Roman and I go way back," Alex says. "And it was no trouble. Well…it was a bit of trouble, Lucia is not a woman I'd want to cross. But we've spoken several times since and her knowledge has been invaluable. I've enjoyed many of our conversations since."

"I'm glad to hear it."

"And she's been amazing for the students."

"Dr. Stevens mentioned the student experience," Roman inserts. "I'm so glad it's worked out all around."

"It has…with the cat too, I see."

My brow furrows, as I blink several times. "The cat?" How would Alex know about Thomasina? "What does that mean?"

There is an awkward pause, the air stilling around us as some energy I don't understand crackles. "I called Alex when Thomasina was in labor," Roman supplies, his hands flexing on mine. "I needed to know if help was required beyond what I could give."

"Oh," relief washes through me because that makes sense. "Right."

"Kitten doing all right?" Alex asks, clearing his throat.

"Hopefully," I answer, still feeling some of the tension that I don't quite understand. "Speaking of, this little one needs to get back to Thomasina. I don't want to open the carrier until we're all contained in the car."

"Right," Roman is already moving us down the hall. "Thanks again, Alex. I'll call you later."

I stroke the kitten in my hand, as Roman opens the door to the clinic and leads us out to the car. He helps me in and then places the kitten in the carrier with Thomasina. Thankfully, she doesn't bolt, content to be with her kittens. "You think the kitten will be all right on the way home?"

I frown, forgetting about Alex, as I look back. "I think eating and being with Thomasina is the kitten's best chance."

Roman gets in the car and pulls out of the lot. "We'll keep an eye on them both tonight."

I nod, drawing in a deep cleansing breath.

Today has been an odd day. Getting back out in the world is everything I've feared and hoped it would be. I've been avoiding the Mikes, but when you face them, you get the moments like the one I had with Dr. Stevens. The great only comes with the bad.

I scratch at my chin, wondering about some of the choices I've made and the ones that are in front of me.

What if I did sell my house? Would I have enough money to finish school? Get a job? Buy a small place to live?

What would my gran really want for me? We never got a chance to discuss it. By the time I realized what was happening, she was too lost to help me find my way.

But maybe I don't need to ask.

Maybe, I already know. She'd want me to make this decision with my head and not my heart.

And if I'm being totally honest, the Kincaids' original offer was beyond generous.

I draw in a shaky breath, my thoughts swirling so rapidly, I almost feel like I can't breathe.

"Maddie?"

"I'm fine. I just..."

"Is this about Alex?"

"Alex? No. Why?"

"Nothing. What's wrong?"

I pack that one away. "I know that Mason already started the process of leasing my yard, but suddenly I'm wondering..." I stop, realizing I'm jumping way ahead of myself. I should order my thoughts first. Is Roman even the person to ask about this?

He takes one hand off the steering wheel and places it in mine. "What are you wondering, my little bird?"

His little bird. I suppose I have been a wounded little creature. But I want to be something else. "Actually, can we discuss it a bit later? I might need to think some more."

"Of course."

I squeeze his fingers, letting out a long breath.

I feel like I'm finding myself again. Or maybe for the first time.

I lean over, brushing my cheek over Roman's shoulder. Whatever happens with Roman, however long he's in my life, I'll always have him to thank for that.

CHAPTER TWENTY-SEVEN

Roman

Coming back to the apartment, I force myself to retreat to my office. First I call Alex. And if I had any doubt, the man is clear. Lucia is completely on the level. A woman of intense passion and strength, she'd never hurt Maddie for the Vendettis.

It makes me feel both better and worse. I'm glad she's a good friend to Maddie. But I used imagined wrongdoings to make some pretty shitty choices.

Shaking off my thoughts, I do some solid work, something I've barely thought about over the last several days, and I'm amazed to find I haven't missed at all.

Even now, I'd much rather be at Thomasina's side with Maddie, staring at the beautiful little kittens.

Jack's words hit me again. Caring for the cat…that makes me feel like I'm doing something good. Not like building a tunnel to connect casinos, which feels nearly pointless.

To be fair, I know the point. Money. Power.

I tip my chair back at the desk, staring at the immaculate top in front of me. I've worked so hard to please my brother, grow the business, fight the war with the Italians; it's been ages since I even asked myself what I wanted.

I like work. I like to be successful, I'm motivated. I want to be busy. But do I like running casinos?

Do I want to be Mason's lackey?

I scrub a hand over my face and push up from my desk.

Heading out to the living room, I find Maddie curled on her side on the floor staring into the whelping box.

"Have you been here the whole time?" I chuckle as I slide behind her, cradling her body against my own.

She leans her head back against my shoulder, a smile tugging at her lips. "I can't seem to tear myself away."

"How's our sick kitten?"

"Fine," she answers. "Eating like the rest of them."

I kiss along her neck, wrapping my arm around her to pull her even closer. She lets out a long sigh.

I know she's got something on her mind. I don't know if it involves me or not. "Nice way to spend the afternoon."

"Good for thinking," she replies.

"Thinking about what?" I start lightly brushing my fingers up and down her arm, trying not to show the tension I feel.

She blows a piece of hair back from her face. "The past, I guess. My present and my future."

I relax, giving her a squeeze. "That's so funny. Me too."

She turns her face toward me, the tip of her nose brushing mine. "What are you thinking about?"

Do I want her to share? I think it might be time for me too as well. "I know you know that both my parents died, but my mom died in a car accident first."

She keeps brushing the tip of her nose over my skin, making it easier for me to keep talking. "She was drunk behind the wheel. She'd gotten a call that I remember. She'd been screaming into the phone, babbling almost incoherently. I couldn't hear the other side of the conversation, but I know what it was about. She left minutes later."

"What was it about? Why did she leave?"

"I think she was going off to catch my dad in his latest affair."

Maddie winces against me, her cheeks pulling taut as her hands tighten on mine. I close my eyes. "The last two years of her life, all she did was drink. All the time. She didn't cook. Didn't clean. When she was really drunk, she'd scream long ranting tirades about my father and his affairs."

She gasps against my cheek. "You're the youngest?"

"No. I have a younger sister. Arabella. She's away at school in New York now. She tries to spend as little time as possible with us, and who can blame her?"

"Mason and Leo. Where were they when all of this was happening with your mother?"

"Leo was already working a casino floor, and Mason was off at business school. Harvard."

"Oh," Maddie's breath rushes across my face. "You were the one stuck taking care of your mother, weren't you?"

"My mother. My sister. The house. Cooking. Cleaning. Walking my sister to school."

"Roman," she turns in my arms, her chest pressing to mine as her arms loop around my neck. "That is so much."

She's not wrong.

"The thing is, I've spent so much of my life doing what other people demand of me. Require. That I haven't asked myself in a very long time what I want. Who I want to be."

Maddie's mouth brushes across mine, the kiss light and comforting. I drink in her taste, her feel, greedy for more.

"And who do you want to be?"

Her man.

Christ, it's so fucking simple. So ridiculously easy. The problem is every move I've made up to this point has made that less and less likely. "Still working that one out."

"Me too," she whispers against my lips. "But I think I'm starting to have some ideas."

"Like what?"

"I don't want to hide anymore, even if people like Mike sometimes hurt me."

I squeeze her tighter. Everyone gets hit by other people's prejudices, but my Maddie is extra vulnerable. "I can go back and punch him out. He deserves it."

She laughs, her chest moving against mine. "I'm all right. Thank you, though."

"What else?"

"I think I want to learn to balance my heart and my head."

"Your heart is one of the best things about you." The words come out before I can hold them back.

She shrugs. "It gets me in trouble a lot. I go rushing in..."

"Maddie, I know. I get it. But it also makes you so lovable. I..." My eyes close again and I roll onto my back, pulling her on top of me. "I love you, Maddie. I'm in love with you."

I feel her breath catch, hear her gasp. Opening my eyes, I stare up at her shocked expression. "Roman."

"I think I know what I want to be too," I murmur and then kiss her open mouth closed.

"What?"

"The person who helps you realize your dreams."

She shakes her head. "No."

"What?" My heart stutters in my chest.

She places her hands on either side of my face. "I know what you're doing. You're taking care of me. Don't. I can do it myself and you've got your whole business. Think about what you're saying."

Grinning, I kiss her again. She's worried about me. Refusing because she wants what is best for me. "Oh. I have." My hands slide down her back and over her ass. Hooking her legs, I pull them apart, settling them on either side of me. "I want you."

"Roman," my name breaks on her lips. But I don't talk more as I kiss her again.

I don't tell her about my fantasy. We run charities, an animal hospital all our own, a rehab center.

We fill our lives with each other, with the care and keeping of all the wounded souls we find—and together, we heal.

Instead, I grind my hips up, pushing her ass down, giving her the sort of pressure that has her frantic in seconds.

Her fingers twine through my hair, our kiss becoming hectic as I part her lips and plunge my tongue into her mouth.

I want to be inside her the way I want to take in air. My tongue, my fingers, my cock.

I want to fill her.

I just fucking want…

Maddie understands, pushing up so that she can yank her shirt over her head. Then she's back on my chest, her skin of her back sliding under my hands.

I snap open the clasps of her lacy bra, the fabric giving. Brushing the straps down her arms, the bra pools on my chest.

I kick off my shoes, not even breaking the kiss, and then reach down and pull hers off too.

She's totally pliant in my arms in this way that I love.

I push her back up, sitting up enough to yank my shirt over my head. When she comes back down, her full tits crush against my chest and I groan in satisfaction.

This is what I need. Her skin on my skin.

Her breath in my mouth.

I'm tugging at her leggings, nearly ripping them off her body. "Roman," she gasps. "You just bought me these."

"I'll get you more, baby." The fabric tears, not that it helps me get them off any faster. But I still try.

Because I don't want her chest off my chest. It takes me some maneuvering and some more tearing to strip her naked.

My own jeans go down much faster.

I don't even care they're still around my knees.

Because my tongue is in her mouth, my cock nestling into her soaking-wet pussy.

Using my finger, I tease her slit, spreading her juices until her hips are chasing my touch.

Maddie is so fucking responsive.

She's already moaning. "Roman. Please. Yes. God."

It only makes me go slower. She grinds harder against me, growing frantic. I love working her into a frenzy and I'd delay even longer, but when she pushes down, the head of my cock sinks through her wet folds and into her entrance.

Now I'm the one moaning out my pleasure as I push in deeper until I bottom out inside her.

I'm still kissing her, swallowing all her noises of pleasure but it isn't enough.

I want more of her.

I want to claim her. Sliding my hand over the crack of her ass, I start a slow rhythm with my cock even as I begin fingering the outside of her little brown hole with my middle finger.

I feel her pussy spasm around me, another flood of her juices running down my thighs and I know she wants it as much as I want to give it to her.

Gently, I push the tip of my finger into her back door, her gasp and then groan of pleasure is all I need to know.

Still. I pull back from our kiss to give her a quick, "You good, baby?"

"So good."

That's all the encouragement I need to sink deeper.

My sweet innocent girl isn't going to last long. I can feel her pussy spasming around my cock, clenching and unclenching as she moans into my mouth, any art with her tongue gone.

It's sloppy and dirty.

It's the hottest fucking sex I've ever had, our bodies so in tune as I pump my tongue, my cock, and my finger in and out of her.

I know she's really getting close when her moans turn to screams.

Wherever we live, Maddie and I are going to need some privacy, because my girl is loud.

She bears down on me, her body growing tight, her fingernails digging into my scalp deep enough I know she's going to leave marks.

But I'm relentless, pumping in and out of her until, she gives one final long, loud cry and then she cums hard.

I feel it gripping me so tight, I nearly break too.

But I hold back.

When her hips finally start to slow, and her head lolls onto my shoulder, that's when I flip her around.

Landing on her back, I only take one second to make sure she's good before I set a relentless pace, pumping in and out of her like a man possessed.

I know I'm claiming her. Maddie is mine.

With every thrust it's like I repeat it over and over.

The cum is boiling in my balls, my body so ready to break, I'm taut as a drum.

That's when I pull out. With a quick jerk, my cum erupts on her belly, showering her with my seed.

I want to see it on her skin.

Her hands are up above her head, her body stretched out before me as she gives me a lazy smile.

Swiping my index finger through the salty liquid, I raise it to her lips, brushing my finger across the plump pink flesh. "Taste me, baby."

She opens for me, her tongue licking along the pad of my finger.

"Just so we're clear," I lay on top of her, my cum now pressed to both her skin and mine as I lick inside her mouth. "I want to be where you are. Doing what you do."

"Roman," she whispers against my lips.

"Let me be your protector, sweetheart. Your muscle. Your eyes when you need to see, your hands when you need precision."

"And in return?"

"You will be my heart. Teach me to love the way you do, sweetheart."

"Oh Roman, you know that already. You always have."

I'm not so sure. Wait until she hears what I've done.

But I can't tell her yet. Frist, I'll make it all right, and then I'll share the whole truth.

Because I need Maddie to stay by my side.

CHAPTER TWENTY-EIGHT

MADDIE

I WAKE THE NEXT MORNING, completely sore and so satisfied.

Roman got up several times in the night to check on the kittens but he made me stay in bed.

He must have moved to the couch at some point, because as I feel along his side of the mattress, only cold sheet meets my hand.

I lift up, swiping the hair from my eyes and turning on my back to swing my feet over the side of the bed.

Roman's place has started to feel like home. "Lights," I call out, the bedroom and closet lights flicker on.

My clothes now hang in the closet, but I move to his side where all his clothes are arranged in a neat line. I never thought I'd be in a closet where my stuff was on one side, a man's on the other.

He has a ton of finely brushed dress shirts. They smell crisp and clean and feel even nicer as they brush my skin.

Reaching for one, I take if off the hanger and pull it on, doing up a few of the buttons at my waist.

Heading for the bathroom, I brush my teeth and toss my hair in a clip before I make my way out to the living room.

Roman is exactly where I thought he'd be, curled up on the couch. He's still asleep.

But at some point, not only did Thomasina decide to curl into the hollow of his knees, between his legs and the back of the couch, she's brought all her kittens there too. Apparently, she got the memo.

Roman is our protector.

I have another moment where I wish I could see this picture more clearly, see Thomasina's expression.

I can hear her gentle purrs. "I'm going to have to put them back in the whelping box, Thomasina," I whisper. "Roman might crush one of your babies on accident."

Thomasina doesn't acknowledge I spoke. Likely ignoring me because she doesn't want to hear what I have to say. Stubborn cat. I softly laugh.

Roman's words from yesterday replay in my thoughts. He told me that he loves me. But also that he wanted me to teach him to love...

I sit down on the floor, my cheek resting on his knee. I think of all the ways he cared for me. He doesn't need me to teach him anything. And I can't let him give up his own career to help me care for homeless animals.

I heard his story about his mother. I've listened to what he's said about Mason. Roman tends to divert his own needs for the people around him.

I will not be one of those people. We'll forge a future together.

Not able to help myself, I reach out and touch the back of his hand, running my fingers along his skin.

He starts under my touch, breathing in deep.

"Maddie?"

"I'm here."

"Miss me in bed?"

"Terribly." I stand up, running my hand gently up Roman's leg and then along Thomasina's body.

I can see the mass of kittens but not their individual outlines. Carefully, I feel for their edges.

"Maddie," Roman growls out, sounding predatory.

I stand up straight, cocking my head. "What's wrong?"

"You look fantastic in that shirt," he rumbles, his hand sliding up the back of my leg and under the hem to cup my ass cheek.

"Do I?" I bite my lips as I run my hand down his arm, loving the feel of his skin under my fingertips.

He sits up, parting the fabric to place a kiss on my belly. "Sexy as hell."

I'm already heating. "Roman," I give a gasping giggle. "We should put the babies back first."

"Your wish is my command." Gently, he lifts the babies, placing them into the whelping box. Thomasina follows and then Roman stands, pulling my body close.

A thrill of pleasure moves through me. His body on mine never fails to erase my thoughts, so that all I do is feel. But Roman and I have some talking to do.

"We ought to take a shower," he murmurs his lips against the shell of my ear.

"That's a wonderful idea. But I also think we need to talk about last night. When you said you wanted to help me realize my dreams…"

He pulls his head back, holding my face in his hands. "I did."

"I appreciate your words so much."

"Maddie, I've got all the money in the world. I can build you an amazing sanctuary. Hire staff."

I squeeze his forearms. "Roman, that's so wonderful. But I think…" I nip at my lip. "There are some things I need to do on my own first."

"Your own?" I hear the worry in his voice. "Maddie, are you ending things with me?"

As if… "That's hilarious. No. I'm not ending anything. Do women usually break up with a man while wearing his clothes?"

"No," he chuckles, his fingers brushing down to the curve of my breast. "And it would be especially cruel with the amount of cleavage you're displaying."

My hand comes to his as I warm all over. "What I meant is that I need to finish my degree. While we continue to have sex. That seems completely appropriate—" His lips on mine cut me off.

When he finally lifts his head, he rumbles close to my ear. "That is a plan I can support."

That's good.

Because it's time I started to learn to walk in this world. Make reasonable decisions and live my life the way most people do. And as much as I'd like to have Roman there to catch me when I fall, I do need to learn to be up on my own two feet.

Later.

Because the moment I think it, he's picking me up in his arms.

He carries me into the shower. I'm well aware that him carting me around everywhere is the opposite of walking on my own but like I said, I'm still in love with Roman. I just don't want him to give me a bunch of things I haven't earned.

I want to learn to be brave and strong. Like he is...

And I'm not taking his future for mine. That's never been my version of love.

He turns on the shower, setting me lightly on my feet, his mouth finding mine.

The kiss is so sexual but also slow, easy. The chemistry is there, but the rush is gone this morning.

His hands trail up and down my body, building a hum as our skin slides together from all the water.

Finally, Roman presses me against the shower wall, and wraps one of my legs around his hips as he eases inside me. Then, he fucks the breath out of me with deep, even thrusts, until I beg him to fuck me harder. Faster. But he never speeds it up and when I cum, somehow, it's even better.

By the time we're done, I'm ready for a nap. Instead, we head into the closet to dress.

I run my hand along my clothes, feeling the different fabrics.

"I've got more work to do," Roman says from his side. "Mason made the public announcement for the final stages of the project, even giving a completion date to the press. The casinos have exploded with traffic."

I turn toward him reaching for his arm and drawing closer so that I can brush a kiss on his shoulder. "Any word on the Vendetti cousin, Luke, or Kate?"

"No," he lets out a frustrated breath. "But. The Andrianis, those are the Italians who are more reasonable, are signing a deal with Mason today. In other words, if the rest of the Italians want to make money, benefit from the tunnel, they have to turn their businesses over to the Andrianis. It should make the rest of the Italians fall in line. And it should send a message to Luke and Kate that's it's safe to come home. Hopefully."

I can hear his worry about Luke. But everything else he said about the business...

It's calculating. Strong. But also…he's shaping events into the form he needs them. Manipulating the circumstances to his advantage.

My hand slips from his arm, and I step to the side, brushing against the clothes hanging on his side of the closet. I touch them to help me think, letting the fabric slide through my fingers.

But my ponderings are short-circuited when, in the pocket of his jacket, I feel something small but firm.

Almost like a…

I reach into the pocket, my fingers wrapping around the case of my phone.

I'd know it anywhere.

My case is distinctive. I picked it for that reason. It helps me differentiate it when several are sitting on a table.

I pull it from his pocket, clutching it against my chest in both hands.

Has Roman had my phone this whole time?

Why?

Why would he have my phone and not give it to me?

My breath catches.

Roman must hear it. He pivots, his bare feet brushing the carpet. "Maddie?" But then his breath draws in on a quick inhale.

"Why is my phone in the pocket of your jacket?"

There is the slightest pause, it crackles in the air. "The police found it in the back of Vigo's car."

I cock my head. "What?"

"Jack brought it yesterday."

I feel the tension. It's the same tension that filled the air when I met Alex.

And I just know...he's lying. He lied then and he's lying now. I can hear the change in his voice. Subtle. I didn't recognize it at first but now... "If the police found it, why isn't it in an evidence locker? Why don't they want to talk to me?"

"Maddie." It's a plea.

I start to shake. He had my phone this whole time. He cut me off from the world, my only access through him.

Tears fill my eyes. "You did this. You kept it from me."

"Maddie," he says again. "It's not like that. Look. I..."

I spin around. I'm only wearing a bra and underwear, I don't even know where I'm going but I sprint out of the closet, banging my shoulder on the door frame.

Roman catches up to me, wrapping an arm around my waist. I scream, trying to tug away. "Sweetheart," he pleads. "Don't run. You're going to hurt yourself."

I feel the tears streaming down my face. "Tell me the truth. Where was my phone? Why did you take it?"

"I wanted to search for Kate's last known location."

I blink back my tears. Because that is a really logical explanation, but it also means that Roman did, in fact, lie to me. What else has he lied about? "Why didn't you just ask me?"

"You were so scared that first night," he tries to pull me close, but I resist, my hands coming to his chest to keep some distance.

It's not that he's wrong. I might have been too scared to hand it over. But also... how can I trust him now? "You lied to me."

"I know, sweetheart. I'm sorry." He does pull me close then, and I let him, though I'm still burning with the agony of betrayal. "I won't make excuses, but we were frantic to find Luke and—"

I blink back my surprise. We? "Mason wanted the phone, didn't he?" Suddenly the fight with his brother in the parking garage makes sense. "That day Mason hit you. Were you and Mason arguing about me?"

Roman is silent. I appreciate that he isn't offloading blame to his brother. But I need to know who to trust.

The silence is so thick, it threatens to break. "Roman please tell me the truth. I have to know if I can trust you."

But before he can answer, my other phone rings, the burner phone that Roman gave me, and Lucia's distinct ring fills the room.

I need my friend so much.

I pull back from Roman and he only holds me for a second before he lets me go.

Crossing to the bedside table, I pick up the phone. "Lucia?"

Can she hear how wrong my voice sounds?

"Maddie," she cries into the line. "I'm going to need you to sit down."

"What is it?" I cry. What else could possibly be going wrong?

CHAPTER TWENTY-NINE

ROMAN

I HEAR the panic in her voice and I'm racing to her side, no matter how angry she is with me.

She has every right to hate my guts. She doesn't even know the half of it, though.

I can't believe I forgot to give her the phone. Things with Thomasina…with her…

I'm forgetting to keep my guard up, forgetting to filter everything I say and do. I'm becoming this totally other person, and the one I am with Maddie.

That man, the man I am when I'm with her, I like and respect.

I'm a better man for being with her.

But the man I was…he's about to ruin everything.

Her wide eyes stare at nothing as she slowly goes to sit on the bed. I can already tell she's going to miss and I reach for her, grabbing her arm so she doesn't fall.

She screams, jerking away, and crashes into the nightstand.

"Shit," I rumble, righting her again.

She goes completely still in my arms. Like a hunted animal. "Maddie?" I ask quietly, dread pooling deep in my gut. "I didn't mean to frighten you, sweetheart. You were going to miss."

"Maddie?" I hear Lucia say into the line. "What happened? What's wrong?"

But Maddie only makes this wounded noise in the back of her throat. "Sit." I quietly command guiding her to the edge of the bed.

She does sit but every muscle in her body is rigid. I run my hands down her arms, trying to help her relax but she flinches away.

I'm afraid she's going to hurt herself again so I drop my hands.

I don't know what's happened, what Lucia said, but I know it's bad.

And I'm worried, by the way she just pulled away, instead of falling into my embrace, that whatever was said, involves me.

Did Alex tell Lucia about Thomasina?

I hear Lucia's voice in the phone, but I can't make out the words.

But by the look on Maddie's face, pain pulling her features taut, I know my world is about to explode.

I drop down on my haunches, my elbows coming to my knees. I try to touch her calf, but she bats at my hand.

"Maddie?" I ask, my voice nearly breaking. "What's wrong?"

"I need your address."

Those words turn my insides cold. "My address?"

"The place that I am. I need to know where that is. I kept meaning to ask. It's so stupid. I don't even know you, why wouldn't I make you give me your address?"

"You know me," I respond, my voice low.

Lucia cuts me off and this time I hear what she says. "If he hurts you, I'll kill him."

Is Lucia talking about me? First of all, I would never harm Maddie. But the idea of Lucia inflicting any damage on me is laughable.

Vincent is a professional killer, and he couldn't take me down.

"Tell me what happened," I try again. If I could just insert some calm conversation into whatever is happening here...

"Address," she cries, her voice breaking on a sob. "Now, Roman."

"Eight-one-one Ash Street."

"Did you hear that, Lucia?" More words from Lucia I can't hear. "No. Don't worry. I'll be fine."

Lucia's voice grows louder so that I hear it. "We're not hanging up, Maddie. I'm worried."

"If I'm not on the street when you pull up, call the police," Maddie answers and then hangs up the call.

The police? Fuck me.

For several seconds we just sit there. Me balancing on the balls of my feet, so tense I'm ready to break, and her, ashen, her features contorted in pain.

I don't want to ask again, and I'm trying to give her the time she needs to calm down.

Her fingers tremble as they slide across her forehead. "Why did a city inspector just serve foreclosure papers to my house?"

I close my eyes. "Fuck."

"Tell me, Roman. Why?" Her voice shakes but I hear the steel in it too. "Why would *you* foreclose on my house?" She emphasizes the word you. She knows.

"Maddie—"

"Don't," she cuts me off. "Try to tell me it wasn't you."

"It was me." I'm not lying to her. Not now. Not ever again.

I hear the sob that escapes her lips. It echoes through me, shattering any composure I have left. My face sinks into my hands.

"So what? You brought me here? Took my phone..." She breaks on another sob. "Then what?"

"Then nothing. I brought you here to keep you safe."

"Taking my house keeps me safe? Explain to me why you would to that?" I wanted to talk, but this is brutal. Still, I owe her the truth.

"The tunnel. You know I need the property to keep the tunnel project moving forward. It's our way to get Luke and Kate back. Fuck—"

She slumps to the side, her face pressing into the pillow as she lets out a wounded noise that rips out my heart.

Tentatively, I reach out to touch her again. I know I ruined everything, but I have to try and fix this. My hand hovers over her body, finally brushing along her upper arm.

This time she doesn't jerk away, but she doesn't pause in her crying either. The tears pour out of her and onto my pillow. I lean forward, resting my face on her legs. "Please."

"What else haven't you told me?"

My teeth clench together. There is a part of me that doesn't want to admit to anything else. But since she knows two of my major sins, I might as well get the third one out. "Thomasina."

She sits up then, so fast, I nearly fall. "What about her?"

"She…Jack didn't find her behind his car."

She smacks my shoulder. Hard. Not that it hurts. And honestly, I deserve for her to give me a good beating.

Pushing me away, she stands. "You manufactured a cat in need?"

"I wanted you to be comfortable."

"You wanted to manipulate me!" She huffs before she spins, charging toward the closet. "Where is my dress?"

"Which dress? You've got like ten—"

"The one I came in. I'll return the underwear I'm wearing later. I—"

"I don't want the underwear back." That's not strictly true. I want the underwear, still dirty, and I want the woman in them. "The clothes are yours."

"I don't want your clothes," she stops, her hands coming to her hips. We've had this entire exchange in our underwear, and it's not helping one bit. I can see every part of her, from her beautifully flat stomach, to the flare of her hips, to her full, round rack. My hands itch to touch her. Hold her close.

"The clothes are yours."

She shakes her head. "It's all been a lie."

"No," I stand too, moving toward her. "I told a few lies but everything else is true."

"How could I have trusted you? How could you…" Tears are streaming down her face, and I hate that I hurt her like this.

I'll do anything to make it better.

CHAPTER THIRTY

MADDIE

I WISH I could have this conversation with Roman and not cry.

I wish my heart wasn't breaking in two in my chest.

But I can feel the tears streaming down my cheeks and my chest aches with all the hurt and pain.

Everything has been a lie.

I was wrong.

The pain in this moment was not worth it. I should go back to hiding in my house. Except that…

This one little adventure out is about to cost me everything.

It takes every ounce of strength I possess not to sink to the floor again. On trembling legs, I carefully make my way into the closet so that I don't bump into anything else. I'm going to be covered in bruises.

Not that I care.

As much as I'd like to retreat to my home and never leave again, I don't even know how long I have before I'm tossed out.

I stop again, drawing in a ragged breath that breaks into a sob. I am the broken bird. The girl with no brains, just bashing her own wings as she flutters into danger with no way of escape. I rushed into this mess with Roman with my foolish heart right on my sleeve.

Gentle hands touch my arms. "Please, Maddie. Don't go. Not like this."

"Why not?" I whisper. "I've got nothing left to give. You've taken everything."

His hands pull away like I've burned them. Is he hurt? That's rich. "The city is not taking your house."

That makes my breath stop in my lungs. "The city would beg to differ."

"I won't let it happen. There is no way."

My throat burns from the tears and I shake my head swallowing down the lump. "Don't make me promises you won't keep."

"I'm keeping this one," he rumbles. "I'm keeping all of them. The one where I promised to care for you. Love you. Your house. The animal sanctuary. All those promises are yours."

I shake my head, his words soothing a bit of my hurt. "How could I ever trust you again?"

"I don't know," he answers back. "But I'd like a chance to try."

The tears have made my already-poor vision so blurred, I can't see a thing. But I hear the hangers rustle. And then I feel his hands on my calves.

"Rest your hands on my shoulders and step into the dress. I'm holding it out for you." I do as he commands because I don't know how else I'm getting dressed.

But I can tell by the feel of the fabric on my foot that it isn't the dress I wore on the date. It's a soft stretchy cotton that glides over my skin.

"Roman," his helping me is not helping. It only confuses me. His care has always confused me. Then again, I'm pretty sure he takes care of people even when he doesn't like them. I think of what he told me about his mother last night.

More tears are falling, but I try to swallow them back as I allow him to close the buttons at the bust. Lucia will be here soon and the faster I'm outside, the quicker this will all be over.

He taps my foot and slides on a ballet flat. And not the ones I came in. "This isn't the clothing I asked for."

"I know, sweetheart, but you're upset. You should be comfortable."

I let out a huff of frustration. "That wasn't your decision to make."

"Other foot." I click my tongue but place a hand back on his shoulder to let him place the shoe on my foot. The really annoying part is that both the flats and the dress are very comfortable and the clothing itself is soothing some of my raw edges.

As are his hands on my skin.

I've gone silent, I don't even know what to say. Thank you? I hate you? I shake my head. What a mess.

Reaching for my hand, he tugs me out of the closet and back into the bathroom. "I'm going to brush your hair."

"Stop." But my voice lacks conviction. "I don't want your help."

"I know what I've broken," he says close to my ear. "And I know you might never forgive me. But let me fix the house first. Right now. Please."

My mouth opens and closes. I don't want anything more from him. Then again, this is a problem he made. It seems fair to let him fix it. "Fine."

"When Lucia gets here, we'll all go to Kincaid Enterprises." He clears his throat. "And just so you know. I didn't keep the address of my place from you to isolate you. I wanted to keep you safe from the Vendettis. They know Lucia, so telling her was a safety threat. I have always wanted to keep you safe. And you are safest with me."

I shake my head. "I can't stay here with you."

"And what about Thomasina?"

My chin notches. "She comes with me. Lucia can help me care for the sick kitten."

"I won't argue." He starts brushing my hair. "I can't stop you from leaving. I won't. But just know, you'll see me camped outside your house until this is all done."

I bite the inside of my cheek to keep my heart from leaping in my chest. He can't mean it.

And I shouldn't be pleased by his words. But some part of me is…

Hair done, he turns away and walks out of the bathroom. I follow, unsure of what to do with myself in the quiet aftermath. Cry more? Yell? Leave and wait downstairs?

He shrugs on jeans and one of the collared shirts I love too much, leaving it untucked.

We're down on the sidewalk two minutes later, just as an Uber pulls up in front of the building.

"Maddie!" Lucia cries, jumping out of the car. She crashes into me, her arms wrapping about me.

I bury my face in her neck. "I missed you."

"Me too," she answers, squeezing me tight.

"Hey man," I hear Josh say. "I'm Josh Anderson, Lucia's husband."

"Roman Kincaid, nice to meet you."

Lucia pulls back. "This isn't a social call, Josh. Don't talk to him!"

"Luc," Josh soothes. "Let's not get carried away. We don't know—"

"It's all right, Josh. I deserve all of Lucia's anger." Roman clears his throat. "Let me pay for the Uber. I just asked Maddie if all of us could go to Kincaid Enterprises to make certain that Maddie's house remains in her care."

"Is that what you want?" Lucia asks me. I can hear that she is still furious.

I nod. "Then we'll have to come back here and get Thomasina and the kittens."

"Seriously?" Lucia lets out a long breath. "This is not how I break up with men."

I've been around for a few of Lucia's breakups. And calmly leaving a situation is not her style.

I find myself holding back a smile as I think of the guy she dated before Josh.

"What kind of breakups do you go for?" Roman asks.

Lucia squeezes my hand. "I'm more of a throw-their-shit-out-the-third-story-window kind of girl."

“Glad we didn’t break up,” Josh mutters.

I never expected to smile in this moment but there it is. The smallest grin pulling at my lips.

Because Josh isn’t wrong.

And having my friends here has added some perspective. Everything seems less crazy and more normal.

Even Roman’s behavior. Roman lied to me as he tried to balance his business and the loss of his cousin and best friend. He manipulated me too. And it was inconsiderate, bordering on mean.

He told me yesterday that he needed me to teach him how to use his heart. His words suddenly make sense and my jaw clenches as I realize something else.

I’m not going back to Roman’s place. I’m going home. But Roman might actually need me as much as I’ve needed him.

CHAPTER THIRTY-ONE

ROMAN

I MAKE the short drive to the Kincaid building, the air in the car thick with tension.

Lucia and Josh sit in the back seat, giving each other several long glances, as they silently communicate with each other.

I already know they're worried.

I've done my best to soothe Lucia since that first phone call. But she knows the man I am now and she isn't going to respond to anything I say.

Funny, just when I started to trust Maddie's best friend, I lost her.

All I can do is prove that I have Maddie's best interest at heart. And one thing I have always been is a man of action. That isn't changing.

And that's going to mean going toe to toe with Mason.

I'm ready.

"Lucia," I say into the silence. "Can you tell me what the inspector said specifically?"

"He said," Lucia lets out a long breath, "that he was foreclosing on Maddie's house by order of the city."

"Anything else?" I remain patient. This isn't my first conversation with an unwilling and angry party. It's part of my job. In the casinos, I can frequently add the words drunk and belligerent to the adjectives used to describe people I'm talking with.

"And that if I had a problem with it, I could take it up with the Kincaids."

My mouth presses into a thin hard line. This is not good. Her eyes meet mine in the rearview mirror and she gives me a hard glare.

"I said that it couldn't be true. That the owner of the house was dating Roman Kincaid. Then he said that you were the man who approached him in the first place and that you were exactly who I should speak with about the foreclosure."

Why would a city inspector, who had taken a bribe, tell Lucia he was affiliated with us? It makes no sense. Tell her to take up the fight with me?

Then my teeth grind together. Unless he was paid a whole bunch extra to specifically mention the Kincaids. To put the blame on me.

I know who did this.

Mason is trying to make certain Maddie and I break up.

Fucker. He is going to pay for this.

I hit the gas, speeding toward the tower and my brother. But before I get there, I spit out a voice command. "Call Charlotte."

Because two can play this game.

My sister-in-law picks up on the second ring. "Roman, what's wrong?"

"What's wrong is that your husband just foreclosed on a blind woman's house, while framing me for it," I spit into the speaker.

Charlotte gasps. "Why would he do that?"

"To close his tunnel deal. To break up me and Maddie."

"Roman?" Maddie whispers, soft and hurt, but Charlotte's gasp tells me that she heard Maddie's voice.

"Charlotte, meet Maddie. Maddie, Charlotte."

"Hello," Charlotte says in the sweet voice with which she speaks to everyone. "It's a pleasure, Maddie."

"Same," Maddie clears her throat. "And I'm so sorry we're meeting, or whatever this is, like this. I've heard a great deal about you. All wonderful."

"I've heard nothing about you," Charlotte replies. "Intentional on Mason's part?" Charlotte asks me.

"I'm sure. I told him that Maddie's interests were taking precedence over Kincaid business, that he needed to treat her like his next sister-in-law, and he took it upon himself to correct the situation by foreclosing—"

"He did not." Charlotte's voice gets sharp in a way I've never heard. "Maddie I'm so sorry," Charlotte adds. "My only explanation is that Luke's disappearance has turned everyone upside down but…" I can hear Charlotte purse her lips. "That is no excuse."

In quick words, I tell her all of it. Mason's plans, Jack's resistance, and my role in the whole thing. I don't leave anything out. I want Maddie to know the truth. Lucia and Josh hear it all too. I hope it starts to mend some bridges. Or maybe it washes them away forever. I intend to be in Maddie's life for a long time and that means being part of Lucia's too. And the only hope I have is with the truth.

Charlotte is quiet until I finish. "What do you need from me?"

"A little help," I grunt. "Even when I quit—"

"Roman," Maddie cries.

I give her a gentle smile to let her know she doesn't need to worry, reaching out to touch her cheek. "You know how stubborn he can be, Charlotte."

"I do." She's quiet and I let her think as I hit a button to open the parking garage gate. "Did I just hear the gate?"

"Yeah."

"Do you want to talk to him first or shall I?" she asks.

"Me first. I'll soften him up with my fists."

"Roman," Charlotte chastises. "Be gentle."

He doesn't deserve gentle, but I don't tell Charlotte that as we hang up.

"Did you really tell Mason to start treating me like his sister-in-law?" Maddie asks, her fingers dancing down the sleeve of my shirt.

I want to kiss that hand, press my lips to each of her fingertips.

"Yes. I did." I lean close, my forehead coming to hers. I know we've got an audience, but I'm pretty sure Lucia needs to hear this as much as Maddie does.

And I'll grovel at both their feet if it gets me Maddie back. "I love you, Maddie Reid. I meant every offer I made. To live my life with you, to love you, to build you a state-of-the-art facility..."

I hear Lucia gasp.

"And I know I messed everything up those first few days. I meant the other thing I said about not understanding how to live life with my heart. Not until you."

Maddie's breath catches again. I reach for her, placing my hand around her neck, my thumb over her fluttering pulse.

"But I promise, sweetheart, if you give me another chance, I'll make it right. All of it. I love you, Maddie. I want to marry you."

"Fucking hell," Lucia mutters. "He's got game."

"Shh," Josh replies back in a voice just above a whisper. "I wish I had popcorn."

Both Maddie and I laugh. It breaks the tension, at least for the moment. Stepping out of the car, I go around and help Maddie from the passenger's seat. Her hands fit into mine. "You're not really going to quit, are you?"

"I am," I answer. "I love working hard but I'm tired of peddling in the business of sin. Jack told me something," I pull her close, wrapping an arm around her waist. "He said I could be bigger or I could be better. I'm ready to be a better man, Maddie. To make a positive difference in this world."

She threads her arms around me. "And I'm ready to make smart decisions instead of emotional ones. Which is why..."

She draws in a breath as I search her face, wondering what she might say next.

But even I'm shocked when she says, "I know I should have taken your original offer for my house."

"Maddie!" Lucia cries. "You love that house."

"I do. But I'd also love to finish school. And get a real job. And..."

Maddie shakes her head. "I know it's too late now. With the foreclosure…."

"It's not too late," I take a chance and bend down to press my lips to hers. "It's definitely not too late. Let's go kick my brother's ass."

"I think you'd better do the kicking," Maddie whispers. "Lucia can back you up if you need it. Fistfighting isn't really my strength."

I laugh again, but as we approach the elevator, I put on my game face. "Josh, if punches start getting thrown, your job is to get Lucia and Maddie out of the way."

"Just Maddie," Lucia retorts. "Maddie meant it. I'll be hitting too."

This is going to be one hell of a business meeting.

CHAPTER THIRTY-TWO

Roman

I watch the floors tick by as the elevator climbs. By the time we've reached floor twenty-five, I've slipped Maddie's hand into Josh's free arm.

I don't want her hurt and I know I'm going to need both hands for this.

We reach the penthouse and the doors slide open.

I breeze past the bustling office, full of lawyers, administrators, and assistants as I make my way to the conference room. It's Mason's preferred place to operate the business.

He sits in the head chair, like the king he considers himself to be, issuing orders.

I don't knock.

And then the doors bang open, and I don't apologize as I stop in the threshold.

A meeting is in progress, several people sitting around the table, including my brother Leo and my uncle Jake.

I draw in a deep breath as I meet Mason's gaze. "Everyone who isn't family, out!"

The other employees instantly rise, but Mason shoots up too. "I decide when meetings are done. Not you."

I cross my arms over my chest, glaring at Mason.

Josh, Lucia, and Maddie are a few feet behind me, hovering in the hall. "Not today, brother."

Mason slashes his gaze over the room. "Everyone stays."

The employees freeze, looking between me and him. We've never argued in front of them before.

Normally, I respect Mason and his authority enough to keep my disagreements private. Not today.

Turning around, I grab Maddie's hand and pull her forward. Tentatively she comes, tucking a stray lock of hair behind her ear.

Jake's wife Nia is also at the table and at the sight of Maddie, she gives a small gasping cry.

"Everyone, this is Maddie Reid. The woman I'm going to marry, if she'll have me." My eyes narrow on my brother. "Today, Mason, our fearless CEO, foreclosed on her house. That is the kind of man you work for."

Leo barks out a laugh and kicks his feet up on the table. "This is going to be fun."

Mason's lips thin. "Everyone out."

"That's what I thought," I respond back.

But as a woman from legal, Addison Winters passes me by, I raise a finger. "Addison, I'll need a place on your calendar tomorrow."

"Of course, Mr. Kincaid. For what?"

"My resignation."

"Roman," Mason spits.

Leo isn't smiling now as Jake pushes up to his feet. Nia's eyes are wide as she looks between me and Mason.

Addison scurries out, the doors closing behind her.

"You are not quitting," Mason starts the moment the doors close.

"That isn't actually your decision." I pull Maddie close, brushing a kiss over her forehead a moment before I look back at Josh. He gives me a nod and steps up to pull Maddie back out of the way.

Lucia moves into the position next to me, her hands balled into fists at her sides.

She wasn't kidding. She plans to be my wingman. Interesting…

But Mason draws my attention again. "Besides being under contract, this is a family business and—"

"I know what the contract says, Mason. I oversaw its development. My name will remain on the letterhead. But I neither have to attend duties or keep my shares. I can sell them to whoever I choose."

Mason spits a string of curses before banging his hands on the table. "You wouldn't dare."

"I told you I was going to marry Maddie. Told you to treat her like family. You. Dared. First."

I start moving closer, my eyes narrowing. "You told me what you thought about my wants and needs. So there is no reason for me to consider yours."

"That's not it, Roman. You weren't seeing clearly. We need that land."

"We got the fucking land, Mason. You were pissed you didn't get it your way. That's it. And I, for one, am tired of you thinking you can have whatever you want whenever you want it. You don't get to ruin everyone else's life for your own benefit."

"A-fucking-men," Leo mutters.

"I won't be your lackey anymore, Mason. I'm done."

"You'll do what I say. You're taking over daily operations when I go back to Colorado—"

"You should talk to Charlotte about that one." I know I'm pushing on his most sensitive point. "I don't think she wants you back in Colorado after what you did."

"You little fucker," he snarls and then he's over the table and rushing at me full speed.

I drop down in a stance, ready for him but he never makes it to me.

Lucia goes low and lunging forward, nails him in the balls.

Mason drops like a sack, pun intended, even as Leo barks out another laugh. "She got him good," he chortles.

"That was for what you did to my friend," Lucia huffs. "And just so we're clear, the shot to the balls you gave her deserved a return hit."

I smile too, bending down to lean over Mason. "The women love you, big brother."

Even in his pain, he punches out, hitting my ball sack too.

Pain lances through me, as I hit the ground next to him. "That was for talking to Charlotte."

I grit my teeth, moaning through the pain. "Your recompense from me for all this shit is still owed."

His eyes roll back in his head. "Calling Charlotte wasn't enough?"

"Not even close."

I get up on my knees, my forehead still pressed to the floor as I try to breathe through the pain. As soon as I'm able, I'll jab him hard in the arm. "Consider that my letter of resignation."

"Even I have to object to you quitting, Roman," Leo calls from his chair. "No one is better at keeping all the details in line, not even Mason. We need you."

I let out a rumble of dissent. This isn't about them. It's about me and Maddie. I blink my eyes several times looking over at her. She's still holding Josh's arm, her eyes wide with fear.

"Maddie would like to sell her house, the full house, to us. Original offer."

"But—" Mason starts. I hit him again. Hard. "Fine," he rumbles.

"I don't want to run the casinos anymore, I need time to help Maddie with her nonprofit. But you could convince me to stay on in the business operations department."

Mason pushes up, his face still etched in pain, but I know he's calculating. "This could work, actually."

That one catches me off guard. "What?"

"Nia can take over the casinos."

"I can," Jake's wife speaks from the table. "And what a powerful message of cooperation that will be for the other families."

"And a nonprofit division for Kincaid will only strengthen our interests and potential deals as developers."

I stare at my brother.

Fucking Mason. He's found his advantage. But I don't care. As long as I have time to help Maddie, I'll be happy. And using Kincaid Enterprises' might and money to further some worthy causes, that is a win/win.

But Maddie doesn't need to stand here and listen to Mason and I hash out the details. "Josh," I finally manage to push my head off the floor. "Why don't you take my car and drive Maddie and Lucia home. I'll join you as soon as I can."

"You want me to take your Tesla?"

I give a single nod. "Yep." I just manage to get to my feet. "Maddie, I'll have all the papers for you tonight for the sale."

She lets go of Josh then and slips into my arms, half supporting my weight. She lifts up on her toes and presses her lips to mine.

Mason pushes up on his feet too. "Maddie, are you next in line for a shot?"

She turns toward my brother with a soft smile. "Of course not, I think we all know I don't possess a warrior heart. I've always just been..." She winces. "Like my patients, I guess."

I see Mason's eyes close. He knows he took advantage of her weaknesses. No man worth his salt ever feels good about doing that to a woman.

Maddie is doing a much better job of making him feel badly than I ever could.

"Maddie, it wasn't personal—"

"It was..." She shakes her head. "But I don't blame you. I wouldn't want my brother to marry someone like me either."

"Maddie," Lucia cries even as my gut clenches into a million knots. I'd rather be punched in the balls a hundred times than hear her say that she wasn't good enough for me.

"That's bullshit, Maddie."

"I know I'm broken, Roman, I've always known," she whispers. "And when you love someone, you think of what they need, not about yourself. I know what you need, Roman, and you, you need someone who isn't so—"

"Do not say it," I feel my throat close. "I need you."

"No. You need—"

"I told you how I'm broken too. Just because my scars are in the inside doesn't mean they aren't there." My whole family is hearing this but I won't hold back from her. Not now.

"But that's exactly why you should pick someone else. Someone you don't have to take care of like you do me."

I stand up straighter, reaching for her, running my fingers down her cheeks. "Did it ever occur to you that what I need, what I've always needed, is someone who doesn't think of herself? Who wants what's best for me?"

"I…" Maddie's eyes go wide.

"And in putting me first, it leaves me free to put her first too without worrying that I'll be taken advantage of."

"Roman," she whispers. "That is so…"

But I pull her close, wrapping her in my arms. My lips capture hers, her arms winding around my neck.

I know we have an audience, but I don't care as I kiss her over and over. Finally, I pull back and speak against her lips. "No one has a better heart than you, Maddie Reid."

CHAPTER THIRTY-THREE

ROMAN

AFTER MADDIE LEAVES, Mason and I get down to business. Not only do we hammer out the contract for Maddie, we start discussing the particulars of transitioning the casinos to Nia and the pieces we'll need to create a nonprofit division.

I don't look at my brother, I stick to the subjects at hand and so does he.

It's not until we're wrapping up all we can do today without paperwork from this lawyer or permits from that city official that he lets out a long breath, "Roman."

"Mason." I square my shoulders giving my brother a hard stare across the table from where we've been working. "Let's not do this today."

"Why not?"

"Because it will end with more bruises."

Leo has been mostly watching us from the corner. He runs the nightclubs so he's well aware of most of the business particulars we've been discussing.

But unlike Leo of old, he seems content to do his part and stay out of any trouble that doesn't concern him.

Marriage suits him unlike any man I've ever met. Which is so fucking crazy, because he's the last man I expected to ever see domestically content.

Mason lets out a long breath. "Look. I'm sorry, all right?"

I stare at my brother. "For which part?"

"All of it. I'm sorry I left you to care for Mom."

"You've already said that."

Leo sits up straighter. "I'm sorry about that one too. Mason has a good excuse, being in Massachusetts putting the pieces in place that built all of this. I was just a fucking selfish asshole who was having fun chasing pussy around casinos."

That puts a half smile on my face. "I appreciate the honesty, Leo."

Mason shakes his head. "In some ways, you held the greatest burden of us all, holding up Mom and Arabella while we were both starting our lives."

I don't say anything, there isn't anything to say. Mason built this business. Leo, he took the brunt of our father's death. We all did our part.

But Mason isn't done. "I thought I was giving you a gift, grooming you to take over." He lets out a long breath. "But when I met Charlotte, I told myself that you were ready to take on a greater role, but it wasn't about you at all. It was about me."

He winces and I know that he is truly sorry and owning up to his part. "I didn't mean to hurt Maddie in my effort to keep you free to run Kincaid Enterprises. But for the record, both of you are capable."

I cock my head to the side, surprised to hear Mason say anything like this.

But Leo fills in. "Now? Now you think I'm capable of taking over? I wanted more responsibility for years."

Mason laughs. "It's funny how you often get what you want when you give up on it, isn't it? I didn't think I'd ever marry..."

"Me either," I mutter as I run a hand through my hair. "But I never wanted to be at the head of Kincaid Enterprises either."

Mason shakes his head. "What you said about selling the casinos… it would be a major loss of revenue."

"And a serious reduction of problems," Leo fills in. "The clubs too. Every time we find ourselves on the wrong side of the law, it begins with a club or a casino."

Mason scrubs at his jaw. "I started with casinos because it was what we knew. We had contacts, family connections. But also, I wanted revenge on the people who killed Dad, I wanted to control the world that crumbled ours." He shakes his head. "But we could let them go."

I nod. "Maybe. Let's wait to make a decision until we know where Luke is. If he's all right…"

"He's all right," Mason whispers and my head jerks up.

"What?"

"I heard from him. He's alive. So is Kate."

All the air rushes from my lungs as I slump against the table, feeling like I just got punched in the gut. "That scrappy fucker." And then a sound like a half groan, half yell breaks from my lips. I'm so fucking relieved.

"Where is he?"

"Colorado," Mason answers. "I'm having him transported to the family compound now. We'll all be together soon."

I open my mouth, not even sure what to say. I get to tell Luke I'm getting married. Get to have him stand next to me…

I feel light enough to walk on water. But before I can ask Mason more details, his phone rings and he picks up before it's even finished a single ring. "Charlotte."

I hear her sharp tone, clipped words. "Sweetheart—" Mason tries to break in.

"But—" he tries again.

"It's not—"

My brows go up. I've never seen Mason unable to get a word in edgewise.

Finally, he lets out a heavy sigh. "It's already done. The house is bought and Leo, Roman, and I are making plans for the future together."

The line is quiet.

"Please come to Vegas, sweetheart. I can't go another night without you."

I've never heard Mason say anything like that either.

Charlotte starts talking again, and I stop listening, about to turn away, when his brow furrows. "Charlotte, I've got to call you back."

He clicks over before Charlotte even responds. "Hello?"

His eyes meet mine going wide with fear.

"What is it?" I spit, my body tensing.

Mason hangs up the phone a second later. "It's Vigo and Vincent. They're out of jail."

"How? There wasn't a hearing."

"Some legal loophole," he grabs his jacket off the back of his chair. "But I think it's best we go get Maddie. She's in the one place the Vendettis know where to look."

"Fuck," I spit as I dial my phone, already sprinting for the elevator. If either of those assholes touch a hair on her head, I'll see them burn in hell.

CHAPTER THIRTY-FOUR

Maddie

I sigh out as I lay back on my bed. I'm only in a towel after my shower, my wet hair settling back on the pillow.

I'll regret it later, but I couldn't resist laying on my own bed.

Everything is familiar in a lovely way but also…

Some brick of disappointment settles in my chest. I'd left this place, had new, scary and exciting experiences. I'd lived life.

It had been painful and wonderful, and as nice as it was to be home, I already missed Roman.

I missed his apartment too and I missed Thomasina.

Though a few of my birds were too damaged to ever return to the wild, none of them were like real pets. Animals that I shared my life with.

I sighed as I turned on my side, lifting my head to prop it on my hand. Was I sleeping in this bed alone tonight?

As much as I'd missed my home, that sounded awful.

I liked having Roman's body wrapped around mine.

I nipped at my lip. Did he really want a future with me? Even now, I questioned it. I'd heard everything he'd said, but was it fair of me to become his wife?

A soft knock on the door had me lifting my head. "It's me," Lucia called from the other side.

"Come in," I answered back, rising off the bed to cross to the dresser.

"Need help?" she asks as she steps into the room and closes the door.

"I'm good," I answer with a smile, but the smile slips. I grab a comfy cotton dress from the closet and move into the bathroom to dress. When I come out with a brush in my hand, I sit on my bed, patting the spot next to me for Lucia to join. "Can I ask you an honest question?"

"Sure," she settles on the bed next to me.

"Why did you befriend me?"

Lucia sucks in a breath. She's older than me, my substitute teacher freshman year of high school. She was looking for extra money over Christmas break. "Because no one has a heart like yours."

We met when I left another class to pick up a wounded bird I'd heard chirping just outside the window. She helped me. "But..." I shake my head. "I require so much from you. It doesn't seem fair."

Lucia laughs, a soft sound as she reaches for my head. "Maddie. I know I'm a lot. Most girls do not punch CEOs of billion-dollar companies in the nuts, FYI."

That makes me laugh. "Mason deserved it."

"Yes, he did." She squeezes my fingers. "When people love me, they love me despite my very obvious flaws. You, my friend, are one of those people. I could ask you, the very same questions you asked me."

I never think of it like that. I see Lucia's good. I don't care about the bad.

"Roman is not too good for you," she says, clearly knowing why I brought this topic up to begin with. "Honestly, he's morally gray at best."

She isn't wrong.

"That's all right, though. I kind of assumed you'd be bad-boy material. You've got enough ethics to make up for the entire Kincaid family, I think. It's why I thought Vigo might be a good fit when we met him that first night."

That makes me cock my head as I consider her words. "I never thought of it like that."

"I know. But please do. Because as much as you are worried about all the physical care Roman will need to give you, you are going to have to constantly make certain that man stays on a clean path. Right his compass in life. He needs you, Maddie, as much as you do him. Promise."

I shake my head, stunned by her words.

"I need Josh to shave some of my rough edges too. And he needs me to get in there and scrap sometimes when he wouldn't. It makes for a good pairing."

I lift the brush and begin working it through my hair. I look calm, but inside I'm hectic. Maybe I needed to come back here, talk to my friend, to see things with Roman clearly.

I do bring value. Value I'd not even considered. Maybe there is a future for us after all.

Excitement pulses through me. Should I call him? Tell him how I feel?

But that's the exact moment my phone rings, Roman's ringtone singing in my ears.

I don't hesitate. I grab the phone. "Roman?"

"Sweetheart." But his voice makes me still. It's rough and worried.

"What's wrong?"

"Have Lucia and Josh pack a bag. Everyone is coming to my apartment."

I gasp even as Lucia grabs the phone from my hand, clicking it on speaker. "What happened?"

"Vigo and Vincent are out of prison. Everyone needs to leave Maddie's house. I'm getting in the car. Mason, Leo and I will be there in five."

Lucia rises from the bed. "Josh," she calls. "We need—"

"Lights out," Josh calls before he opens the door to my bedroom, closing it behind him.

That's when I hear the roar of the Lamborghini engine.

I'd know that car anywhere.

Vigo and Vincent are here.

CHAPTER THIRTY-FIVE

Maddie

"Is the front door locked?" I whisper.

"Yes, but..." Josh grabs both my hands, pulling me up from the bed. I've got a small walk-in closet, and he pulls both me and Lucia toward it. "It's not going to keep them out for long."

"I don't want to hide," Lucia hisses. "I'm going to—"

"No." I shake my head even as Josh closes the closet door. "Vigo and Vincent are not like Mason and Roman who would hold back. They're not morally gray, they're black. You'd get a good shot in, Lucia, and then they'd break you apart."

Lucia harrumphs but I know she heard me because she stays in the closet.

Even through the door and the walls, I hear the engine cut. A sheen of sweat breaks out on my skin as I try to force myself to remain calm.

Roman is coming.

Of course, the last time he met Vigo and Vincent at my house, he and his cousin ended up shot.

And I know he's not wearing a bulletproof vest today.

A small whimper falls from my lips. Josh, Lucia and I are huddled together and at the small noise I make, we all press closer in.

A pounding starts on the door. "Maddie," Vigo calls. "I'm home. Miss me?"

"Fucker," Lucia mutters. "You got anything that could pass for a weapon in here?"

I frown. "An umbrella maybe?" I whisper back.

"Let me in, sunshine, so we can talk." Vigo pounds some more.

I draw in a stuttering breath. "He can't know we're here, can he?"

"I like your shiny new car," he says as he keeps banging. "But how does a blind woman drive a Tesla?"

"Shit," Josh says.

Here I am again. Vigo knows I'm here.

Last time, I answered the door. This time...

"Think we should go out the back?" We're trapped like rats if we stay in this closet.

"How long until Roman arrives?" Lucia shifts, like she's looking at her watch. In the dark of the closet, I can't see anything.

"A few minutes."

Josh lets out a long breath, but the sound is interrupted by Vigo kicking the door. It holds, but barely.

We don't even say the words, we just move back to the door, opening the closet.

The door to the backyard is right next to my bedroom, the hall keeping us blocked from view.

"Make sure Vincent isn't waiting at the back door," I hiss, Josh slowly turns the knob.

"It's clear," he mutters and we all step into the late-afternoon heat.

It's a covered veranda, where I would keep most of my animals. The fans are off since the yard is empty, which means I can hear Vigo's assault on my front door.

I hear the creak of wood above and I look up, seeing the blurry outline of a person.

"Mrs. Higgins," Lucia hisses waving her hand, "come down!"

My upstairs neighbor. Who is deaf…

I wave my arms wildly, gesturing to her to come but I have no idea if she sees my efforts or not.

The front door gives, the sound of wood splintering echoing down the street,

We all duck down, heading for the small back gate that's hidden by a few overgrown bushes. It leads into a back alley, and Josh shoulders the gate open just as I catch the scent of gasoline. "No," I turn back toward the yard and Mrs. Higgins on the stairs, just in time to hear the ignition of gasoline converting to fire…

CHAPTER THIRTY-SIX

Roman

Leo speeds round the last corner to Maddie's house, the Civic taking the corner like it's on rails, as Vigo's bright yellow Lamborghini comes into view.

Vigo is kicking at the door while Vincent...

Fuck.

He turns from the trunk, a very large weapon in hand. I don't even get the chance to identify the rifle before it's showering us with bullets.

But Mason wasn't wrong. This car is built like a tank. It takes every shot, as Leo jacks the breaks.

"Jesus," Leo roars, the car skidding out sideways as he tries to stop.

It barely misses Vincent, crashing into the back left side of the Lambo.

Vincent recovers first grabbing a gas can from the back of the car.

I see it and I know what he's going to do.

Hitting the window button, I pull out my pistol. Amazingly the window still works, even as I level the gun and shoot.

Not at Vincent but the gas can. Fuel spills to the ground even as he throws some on the hood of our car.

"Fucking reverse," Mason booms from the back seat.

Leo throws the car into gear and jacks the gas, the car careening back, bumping over what I can only guess is a busted front tire.

But I don't take my eyes off Vincent.

I've always known the Vendettis were unhinged.

But even I'm not prepared for Vincent to fire up his lighter, still holding the leaking gas can.

He raises the Bic over his head like he's going to launch it at us but I watch his sleeve catch. Like lightening, flames engulf his clothes. "Stop," I boom. "Stop the car."

Leo hits the breaks again and I'm out in a second, rolling on the pavement.

This began with the death of Vincent and Vigo's uncle, Nia's father.

But it doesn't end with more killing. Shrugging off my jacket, I race toward Vincent, ready to douse the flames.

That's when the gas can catches though.

I see it a second before it blows and I drop to the ground, my hands covering my head.

I hear Vincent's scream, Vigo's war cry.

Lifting my head, I see Vigo racing to his brother's rescue. "Vigo, no! The car!"

But he doesn't listen.

And that's when I hear another distant cry from the backyard. Maddie.

I'm on my feet in a second, sprinting toward the wall. Just as Luke did, I vault myself up and over, the roar of an explosion filling my ears as the car blows.

I have no idea what carnage is behind me.

I don't look. In the very back of the yard, I see Maddie, partially hidden between two bushes. "Sweetheart!"

"Roman," she cries, pointing toward the house. "Mrs. Higgins!"

I turn to see the old woman crouched on the stairs.

Smoke billows through the air as I pivot, sprinting up to her and grabbing the old woman in my arms. I barely stop as I head straight for Maddie.

"We have to get out of here," she cries as soon as I'm at her side.

Looking back over my shoulder, my heart stops in my chest.

The house has caught on fire too. It's going to burn...

I look back at Maddie, a tear slipping down her cheek.

"Come on, sweetheart." With Mrs. Higgins still in my arms, we step out into the alley, the sound of sirens already filling the early-evening air.

CHAPTER THIRTY-SEVEN

MADDIE

IT TAKES hours to sort out the police and the other emergency services.

My house is mostly gone.

It's a good thing I've got a buyer, and he's assured me he's not backing out of the deal. And I'm talking about Mason.

He's even got papers for me to sign in the morning, but the weird part is, I'm not even worried.

Roman is not going to turn me out onto the street. I even hear him whispering to Mason about letting the insurance come through before the sale.

Not that it matters.

I'm pretty sure I'm marrying a billionaire. Once we're all done at the police station, Lucia, Josh, and Mrs. Higgins are shuttled into a limo and taken to Roman's apartment building.

While we've been busy being questioned, Mason's assistant has seen that two other apartments have been outfitted with basics. A bed, linens, a couch in each, and bar stools at the island.

Roman hands a set of keys to Mrs. Higgins and then another to Lucia.

"How much is the rent?" she asks, taking the key and unlocking the door. When it swings open, I hear her gasp, "Do you see those windows?" Wait until she gets a look at the bathroom.

"Lucia. This is not a rental, you're welcome to stay as long as—" Roman starts but Lucia cuts him off.

"I'll never move out, if you continue to talk like that."

"What my wife means," Josh inserts, "Is that we would never take advantage of your generosity and as hard-working adults, we'd feel better paying rent."

"We're not billionaires, though," Lucia adds. "And being a vet is not the same as being a doctor. As you think of numbers, bear that in mind."

I smile, hiding it behind my hand. After a long night, it's so nice to have a bit of banter, but also…my smile turns into a yawn. "How about we discuss the particulars of rent in the morning? I'm exhausted."

Roman's arm comes around me, his lips grazing my forehead. We make our way to the elevator as I count three floors until we reach the penthouse. I laugh to myself. Roman has created a nice buffer between us and them for very obvious reasons.

We don't say a word as we make our way into the bathroom, Roman turning on the shower as I start to strip off my clothes.

I hear him shrug off his jeans and shirt before his hand clasps mine, pulling me into the hot spray.

Tired as I am, I don't hesitate to press my body to his, winding my arms around his neck as his lips find mine.

"Oh Maddie," he rumbles against my lips. "I was worried, after the house, you'd change your mind."

I sigh, shaking my head before I kiss him again. "I can't believe both Vigo and Vincent are dead."

"I'm not crying over it," he says squeezing me tighter. "But I didn't actually want them dead either. Even after everything."

I thread my hands into his hair. My billionaire bad boy is learning to use his heart. "Me either."

"Still, it'll be easier for Luke and Kate to come back with them gone..."

I nod. Roman told me hours ago that Kate was alive. "I know I only knew Kate for a night, but I'd take her coming back over my house."

He squeezes me tighter. "That's why I love you, Maddie."

"I love you too." So much.

His hand trails down my spine. "You know...I have asked you to marry me...a couple times now."

I smile kissing him with all the passion building inside me. "My answer is yes."

"Thank fucking God." He lifts me into his arms, my legs wrapping about his waist as his cock nestles into my folds.

I'm already wet but Roman spits into his hand, rubbing the spit at my entrance before he pushes inside me.

My back arches as I take him in, a needy moan falling from my lips. "When do you want to get married?" he says even as he pumps into me.

It's either the best time or the worst time to have this conversation. I can barely think as I tug at his hair. "I don't know. Everything has been so fast. We can take our time with the wedding, can't we?"

"Agreed," Roman slows the pace, kissing me long and deep. "Tomorrow we shop for a ring, though?"

I nod. I am absolutely fine wearing a piece of jewelry that tells the whole world I'm engaged to Roman Kincaid. "Definitely."

"Anything you really want?"

I lean back, biting at my lip. The sparkle of jewelry is mostly lost on me. "I trust your taste."

His hands are on my hips as he lifts me up so that I slide back down his cock, so full, I moan again.

"A sapphire, I think, vintage."

I gasp at the thought of a dark blue stone, a color I'd be more likely to see than a pale diamond. And old with a bit of dinge is so me. It's perfect.

We don't talk as Roman picks up the pace, working my body until I explode around him.

When we finally get out of the shower, we collapse onto the bed, and I fall instantly asleep on his chest.

For a day filled with so much bad, there has also been so much good.

Lucia is just a few floors away, I'm safe from the Vendettis forever, and I'm marrying the love of my life.

How could things get any better?

EPILOGUE

Maddie

One year later...

The Colorado sun fills the large family room with so much natural light, the shape of the pine trees in enough contrast that I can make out their edges.

This is our…vacation house? Getaway?

I'm not totally certain but I have to be honest, I love it here. I can't wait to be here when it snows.

We've just finished the construction of the rehab center on the outskirts of Vegas. And I took a few classes last semester.

It was amazing to be back in the classroom, to think of finishing my degree. But with construction done and school out, it seemed like the perfect time to get away.

The planners are coming in less than an hour and since Roman has stepped back from the company, he's thrown himself into every detail of the build of the new center—and our wedding.

Honestly, he's a man who likes to work hard and keep track of infinite number of details.

I know all the reasons he's furious with Mason, but I hope they make up. Roman should be working for Kincaid and I worry he'll grow bored with our life.

Which is why it concerns me when he leaves right before the planners. It's not like him and it makes me wonder.

Has he changed his mind?

I know I'm prone to insecurity, but this time...

I hear the front door open and close, the sound of Roman's footfalls joined by some soft tapping.

Fiddling with the ring on my finger, I rise to see what Roman has brought with him today.

"Roman?"

"Coming," he answers. I wasn't surprised when he said he wanted to go to Colorado. It's hot as Hades in Vegas, and Colorado is so much more beautiful in the early summer.

But I was a bit suspicious when he said he had an errand to run this morning.

We've got wedding planners coming in less than an hour.

We're finally getting married and we've decided to have the ceremony here. It's so beautiful, the smell of the forest alone fills my senses.

It will be just intimate family and friends, which I thought meant very simple but, Roman is Roman.

He's planning every detail right down to the weather, I'm fairly certain. Which is why him leaving before the planners are set to arrive is odd at best.

That's when I hear the panting.

Thomasina hears it too, and she gives a howl and then a hiss.

Her feet scamper away and I'm sure she's hiding.

From what?

I turn the corner to the entry, the morning sun streaming into the room.

Roman is there, I know the cut of his shoulders anywhere.

And next to him…

"Is that a dog?" I stop as my hands cover my mouth.

"Meet Birdie."

"Birdie?"

"I hope you don't mind that I named her."

My hands crop to my sides as I lower myself to the floor. "You named her?"

"Birdie is a nine-month-old Seeing Eye dog in training. She's passed her initial tests."

"Roman…" I look at my husband even as a wet nose presses to my face. "What have you done?"

Roman squats down too, linking his hand with mine. "I know you want some more independence. Birdie can help with that."

"But I've been on the list for years, I…"

"It was easier in Colorado," he whispers back. "And there are some perks to dating a guy like me."

I know he pulled strings to get Birdie. The dog snuggles her face right into my chest and I run both my hands down her ridiculously soft fur. "What happens if she doesn't do well with the training?"

"Our choice. We can keep her or wait for the next available pup."

I scoff. I love her already. "She stays."

Roman laughs. "Actually, she has to attend training. But I thought you'd want to meet her first. And she's my wedding present to you so…"

I laugh. "You cad."

"I'm a cad? For getting you a dog?" My eyes are misting over. Birdie is so perfect. Even her name…

"It's not fair how good you are at giving presents." But honestly, I've got a really good one for him too.

We've never been great with birth control.

Rising up from the floor, Birdie follows me into the kitchen where I grab my purse from the counter.

Opening it up, I pull out the tiniest little reem of glossy paper.

Roman has followed too. "You know, you ought to warn me before you give me large gifts."

"Sorry, sweetheart," he rumbles. "Next time. Promise."

I shake my head. "Lucky for you, I came prepared." And then I hand him the little slip.

"My gift to you. It isn't a dog but..."

I hear him unroll the sheet, his breath stuttering. I hold mine, waiting for his response.

"Maddie," he rumbles, the sound so low and deep, I cock my head. I hope he's happy. I can't tell by his tone. We haven't really talked about kids. It's been all rehab center and wedding.

Neither of us had the best childhood, but I kind of assumed... "Are you upset?"

"Upset?" he asks, but I still can't read his voice.

"I know we didn't plan it, it just kind of happened but..."

His arms come around me and suddenly I'm spinning in the air. Birdie barks excitedly, and from somewhere in the house, I hear Thomasina howl.

"Sweetheart, I'm thrilled." And then he kisses me, long and slow and sweet. My hands come to his hair as I lose myself in his kiss.

Our family is growing, everyday a new amazing adventure.

I couldn't be more thrilled...

KING OF PAIN

A billionaire bad boy in disguise
A med student with nothing left to lose…

Powerful
Gorgeous
Sexy as sin

The moment I find Luke Kincaid bleeding and broken, I know he's trouble. He opens his eyes, takes one look at me, and utters a single word.

"Mine."

Maybe I should have run right then.

But he's also the only man who can hold back the dark shadows of the Las Vegas underworld that have found their way to my door. So when I run, he provides the shelter, wrapping me in his strong arms.

It feels natural…right to give him everything. My time, my heart, my virginity. It's not until after that I realize it's all been a lie. He's nothing that I thought he was. But now…I'm hooked.

Rock. Meet hard place.

Even knowing that he's dismantling my life brick by brick, I can't turn away from a single touch.

He's going to ruin me. Or save me. I still don't know, but I'm not sure it matters.

Because every brush of his fingers is lightning, every kiss thunder…. Our passion is a storm.

And I can't get enough.

KING OF PAIN

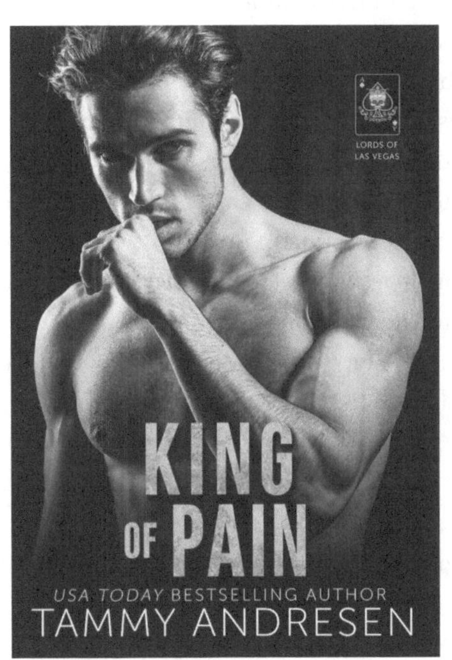

Luke

The trunk of a fucking car is no place to get my bearings.

Bleeding from a bullet wound doesn't help.

I blow a frustrated breath through my nose, but I don't pound on the lid of the trunk, no matter how much I'd like to vent my rage.

It won't help and it will just burn up my energy. This is a moment for control if I'm going to escape.

I should have known this was coming. The shit my family has been in lately…

Just to get this out there, and in case it wasn't clear, I'm not one of the good guys.

The car, a Lambo, and yeah, trunk space is tight in those fuckers, takes the corner at full speed and I crash into the side.

That fucker Vincent did that on purpose.

Vigo and Vincent Vendetti are the reason I'm stuffed into the trunk of a car with a bullet wound. They are the reason for a lot of my family's problems lately.

I grit my teeth and try to brace myself.

The car takes another corner, but I hear the engine downshift before the clank of a gate fills my ears.

I catalogue the details as the car finally stops. We've been driving for at least thirty minutes, putting us well outside of Vegas. I think.

One, two doors open and close before I hear a third and then…the whimpering of another person.

Fuck. That isn't Vigo or Vincent, that's for damned sure. The sound is high and clear like the cries of a woman.

The trunk opens and Vincent hauls me out. It's got to be two in the morning, the darkness thick and inky beyond the ring of the house lights.

Just to my right, a woman kneels on the ground, a curtain of long dark hair covering her face. But it doesn't hide her shivering, or the pretty dress she wears. What the fuck?

I just get my feet under me when he pushes me to the ground waving a gun in my face, as he spits out the words, "Here is how it's going to go, you murdering piece of shit."

Now there is the pot calling the kettle black. I'm no saint but I've never put a woman in a dress like that on her knees. All right, that's actually bullshit. But I haven't done it to hurt her. If she's on her knees, we're both enjoying it.

"You..." He points the gun at the woman. "Are going to patch him up. Fortunately for him, and you, we need him alive."

She doesn't say a word.

"To what do I owe this unexpected show of mercy?" I ask, spitting on the ground right at his feet.

Vigo bends down, looking me right in the eyes. "I had the best date tonight. Gorgeous woman with a very interesting piece of real estate right in the heart of Vegas. I hear it's the perfect location to vent an underground tunnel meant to connect several casinos."

Fuck. Of course I'm here because of the tunnel. And if I were better at my job, we'd already be in the final phase of construction. "You need me alive to date some chick?"

"No, I need you alive so that your family stops chasing permits and starts chasing you, instead." He grins right in my face. "And when those permits don't go through, you can sign over the unfinished project to me."

I didn't think Vigo was that smart. He's gotten several details right that I wouldn't have given him credit for. I am the one in charge of the tunnel project, and without me, my family will scramble to close the deal. They never should have left me in charge in the first place.

The only thing I can do now is make this fucked-up situation right. Which means getting the fuck out of here.

The woman next to me has her chin down, little sobs escaping her lips. I can see her bare knees digging into the stone of the drive.

"And you, cutie," Vincent uses the hand not holding the gun to lift her chin and force her gaze to his, "are going to fix him up and then you're going to join me for the rest of the evening."

She whimpers, shrinking as I push up onto my knees. She looks over at me, a quick glance in my direction is all it takes. "No. Please."

Her voice is small and scared, the tone of it, skating down my spine. I catch her eyes and I have the strangest thought. He's not touching her.

"Mine," I rumble out low and deep before I stop myself. Where the fuck did that come from?

Maybe she doesn't hear me, or maybe Vigo and Vincent scare her too much to lift her head again. I'm not sure she's hearing anything the way she's trembling. But I shift closer, gritting my teeth.

Vigo points a second gun at my temple. "Don't move, asshole."

Vincent gives me the barest glance before he bends down, getting right in her face. "I paid for fucking dinner, you put out."

The Vendetti twins wear matching bad suits, their V-neck T-shirts clearly visible under their open jackets.

Vincent crops his hair short, making his large nose even more prominent while Vigo wears his longer, slicked back from his face.

They both look like pricks to me, but my cousin, Arabella, once told me they hold a certain appeal. I don't see it.

And my guess is, if this girl ever found Vincent handsome, she doesn't now…

Vigo hauls me to my feet, wrenching my injured arm, as Vincent wraps a hand around the girl's upper arm, half dragging her up and onto her stilettos.

We don't go up the massive front steps of the gaudy McMansion, so in line with everything else about these two Italian gangsters.

Instead, we're dragged around back. My legs are starting to work again, the cramping from the car receding.

And despite the bullet wound, my muscles twitch to fight. Vigo walks just behind me with a gun to my back. Vincent in front of me as he half drags the woman, her heels wobbling as she tries to keep up.

My eyes survey the large brick wall that encloses the property and sweep back to the iron gate with a guard.

This isn't the moment.

They pull us toward a small guest house on the edge of a massive pool. Vincent goes first, dragging the woman inside, Vigo, with a gun still to my back, shoves me inside next.

"Supplies are in the back. You've got an hour," Vincent snarls before the door closes and locks.

I stare at the door.

What the fuck? They're just leaving us here? I'm still on my feet. "What is that guy on?" I mutter, looking at the woman who has sunk to the floor once again. She's got her arms around her middle, small sobs escaping her lips.

Fuck me. Two crazy fucking twins, a bullet wound, and a hysterical woman I've already half decided I'm taking with me when I go. Could this night get any worse?

"Hey there, love?" I run my hand over the bloody mess of my shoulder.

She doesn't say a word.

"Why do Crazy One and Crazy Two think you can patch me up?"

Fuck me. She whimpers again, looking so frightened and so fragile. I'm going to have to calm her down. I do not have time for this.

But also, not leaving a massive blood trail would be helpful. I crouch down. "I'm Luke. Nice to meet you."

Her head lifts. There's only the dimmest light from the glow of the pool just outside, but I see the shine of her dark eyes, the tiny nose, the full lips. She's also got a fair bit of really gorgeous cleavage on display. "Kate." No wonder my first reaction was lust.

And now we're getting somewhere. "Hi, Kate. What brings you here this evening?"

She stares at me like I'm the crazy one. Probably valid. So I try again. "How did you end up in the Vendettis' car?"

"You know them…" is all she says as she shrinks away, beginning to scoot backwards on the floor.

"Love," I murmur low and gentle. "There is no need…" But I stop as she vehemently shakes her head, sliding back until her back hits the couch.

I sit my ass on the floor too, trying again. "Judging by the dress, you were on a date?"

"I…" she swallows, her voice cracking. "I just wanted a nice dinner. I…"

I'm going to have to negotiate this one very carefully. "Kate," I say even more softly. "I'm going to try and get us out of here. But first, I'm going to need you to look at my shoulder."

She blinks several times, tears still falling down her cheeks. "Don't let him take me into the house."

I jerk my chin in agreement. "I won't." I can't even explain why I'd make a promise like that, but I do. If I'm going to fight though, first I need her to bandage the bullet wound...

She slips off her shoes, setting them carefully to the side before she pushes to her feet.

Her knees are scraped, her arms bruised. But she brushes her hair back from her face and starts toward a closed door.

She opens it, checks what is clearly a closet and then looks in another. Finding the bathroom, she enters.

Thirty seconds later she returns with a decent-sized first aid kit. "I'm going to wash up," she doesn't look at me. "I'll need you to strip from the waist up."

I try to unbutton my shirt but my arm just won't lift like that. I hear the water turn on. Waving my good arm, I flag her down. "Kate." She looks back at me. "Before you scrub up, any chance you can..." I gesture to the row of buttons. I could do it. But I'm trying to conserve the arm for when we might really need it.

She lets out a long rush of air. "Right. Yeah."

Padding back over to me, she stops just in front of me. I can actually smell Vincent's shitty cologne on her, but underneath that....

She smells like the ocean and lilies. Floral with a bit of salty musk that makes my teeth grind. I breath deeply even as her deft fingers work down my row of buttons.

"You a nurse?" I try again.

With sure hands, she takes the shirt off my wounded shoulder. "I'm in med school," she answers softly. "Just finished my first year."

"Oh yeah, so a real dummy then?"

A faint smile touches her lips before she gasps at the sight of the bulletproof vest I'm sporting. Her hands drop and she takes a giant step back.

"The vest isn't going to hurt you."

"Are you?" she asks, her eyes wary as she assesses me. She's got these gorgeous cheekbones and large brown eyes, fringed with dark lashes. Full lips and a delicate shape to her face. She looks so vulnerable. I want to pull her close.

"No," I answer quietly. "And you're going to have to trust me on that. We don't have much time."

She grimaces, but nods, and then helps me take off the vest too. And last, comes my T-shirt. I can see a rip, the sleeve soaked in blood.

She grabs the hem, her pretty little hands sliding up my skin as she takes the fabric off my good arm first.

It hurts but I ignore the pain, watching her remove the shirt with slow care that hits some note deep inside me. Gentle and beautiful...

The shirt finally comes off and I look down at my shoulder, relief rushing through me. It hurts like hell, but it looks like the vest caught the worst of the bullet.

Kate returns to the sink, washing her hands. She opens the kit, assesses the contents, and washes her hands again, before putting on gloves. "Come sit."

I take one of the two kitchen chairs, as she bends over me and begins to inspect the wound.

I'm less worried now that I've seen the injury, and her cleavage is fucking fantastic. I hold still until she pushes right on the wound and then I hiss in a breath.

"I see the bullet in the vest. I think the edge of the metal cut your skin good, and you'll have a lot of bruising but..."

"I didn't actually get shot."

She shakes her head, that silky hair brushing over her shoulders. Returning to the first aid kit, she pulls out gauze and tape, and some butterfly stitches, making quick work of the job.

But she's still working when the door bangs open again.

It's fucking Vigo.

He stalks in, smirking at me even as Kate ducks behind me. I stand, blocking her from view.

"Think he's going to save you, Katie?" He sneers. "Think again."

Another man comes in behind Vigo. I assume it's Vincent and draw in a deep breath, widening my stance.

But Vigo only smiles wider. Crazier.

"This is my cousin, Guerriero. He's going to keep you both company. He doesn't speak a lot of English so I wouldn't bother begging." Then Vigo spins, saying something in Italian, before the door closes again and the lock clicks.

The other man glares at me, his eyes hard, his bulging muscles, I'm not going to lie, flex impressively. "That's what 'roids will do for you," I say as I reach back for Kate's hand.

She slips her small silky fingers into mine, pressing to my side.

"Where…you…go?" Guerriero asks, his accent thick.

"Don't worry, Gorilla," I give him a toothy grin that's meant to make me look like the predator I am. "The lady needs to change. We'll BRB." And then I start toward the small room I see next to the bathroom.

"What you say?"

I don't answer as I go by Guerriero, who pivots to watch us, and I pick up both my shirts as we pass. "If you can't find anything else we can put one of my shirts on you."

"They're soaked in your blood."

I look down at her, one of my brows rising. "Trust me, covering that cleavage is worth a bit of blood."

She gasps, even as I tug her toward the pool changing room.

There isn't much but there is a robe and a set of men's swim trunks. She wraps the terry cloth around her, cinching the belt tight.

I know we've only got a minute. I'm surprised that ape hasn't tried to stop me already.

In the corner, I find a pair of flip flops and toss them to her.

They've got to be three sizes too big as she slips her tiny feet in them, but at least they're better than those heels.

"Where you?" Guerriero growls.

Tucked in the back of the changing room, I see another door. Softly opening it, I find another room with several pool supplies. A skimmer, a pole, and a longass string likely used for one of the pool covers. It's my lucky fucking day.

That's when I grin. And I probably look like a crazy person too. Because Guerriero and I are about to tangle.

"Kate. Love," I whisper. "I'm going to need you to hide."

Want to keep reading? King of Pain *is next in the "Lords of Las Vegas!"*

Have you loved the series? Don't worry! After King of Pain, there is one more book, King of Deception. Gris Smith is ready to win your heart...

STALK ME LIKE AN ALPHA!

Join my newsletter to get all the latest updates!

Tammy's Newsletter

And follow me everywhere else for teasers, giveaway, book news and fun!

www.authortammyandresen.com
www.facebook.com/authortammyandresen
www.instagram.com/tammyandresen
https://www.tiktok.com/@lordsoflasvegas
www://amazon.com/authortammyandresen

MORE ABOUT TAMMY

Tammy is the writer of Bestselling Regency Romance who could not resist the urge of writing in the dark and delicious world of Contemporary Dark and Steamy Billionaire Romance.

She lives with her husband and three children in Massachusetts and her favorite adventures are the ones that are found in books but occasionally she lives a few of her own!

Made in United States
Troutdale, OR
05/26/2026

49522559R00136